DOCTOR WHO
THE SPACE PIRATES

DOCTOR WHO
THE SPACE PIRATES

based on the BBC television series by
Robert Holmes
by arrangement with BBC Books, a division of
BBC Enterprises Ltd

TERRANCE DICKS

Number 147 in the
Target Doctor Who Library

TARGET

published by
the Paperback Division of
W H Allen & Co Plc

A Target Book
Published in 1990
By the Paperback Division of
W H Allen & Co Plc
Sekforde House, 175/9 St John Street, London EC1V
4LL

The BBC producer was Peter Bryant
The director was Michael Hart
The role of the Doctor was played by Patrick
Troughton

Printed and bound in Great Britain by
Cox and Wyman Ltd, Reading

ISBN 0 426 203461

Contents

1

Spacejack

Beacon Alpha One hung silently in the blackness of space, its complex shape recalling the technology of distant Earth.

On that far-away planet the beacon's different segments had been carefully constructed to withstand the rigours of long years in deep space. They had been ferried to this isolated spot on the edge of the galaxy by space freighter, and painstakingly assembled by skilled engineers. Held together by magnetic force and packed with complex computerized instruments, the beacon was one of a chain of lonely sentinels in space that fulfilled vital navigational functions.

Men had expended thousands of hours and millions of galactic credits to put Beacon Alpha One into position.

Now other men were coming to destroy it.

The sleek, black, dart-shaped ship slid smoothly up to the beacon like a killer shark approaching the belly of a basking whale. It locked smoothly on to the beacon's airlock with a precision that spoke of skilled piloting.

A hatch slid open inside the beacon. Three space-suited figures came through, each carrying a small black box. Their leader, a tall, thin, worried-looking man called Dervish, crossed to a hatch on the other side of the airlock and swung its locking-wheel. The three men filed through into the interior of the beacon.

More space-suited figures were busy outside the beacon, floating across its surface and attaching magnetic charges at carefully chosen weak points. Others were clamping small propulsion units to different segments of the beacon's hull. The team worked swiftly and efficiently in full radio silence, as if carrying out a familiar, often-rehearsed operation.

A lean, dark, sharp-featured man called Caven appeared in the airlock doorway. 'Dervish? Dervish, where are you man?'

Dervish appeared hurriedly from inside the beacon. It wasn't wise to keep Caven waiting.

'We've just about finished,' Dervish said defensively, before Caven could speak.

'About time.'

'The men are just coming back – we'll detonate by radio beam.'

Dervish cursed himself for babbling even as he spoke: he was saying things that Caven knew perfectly well, but somehow Caven always made him nervous.

'Hurry up,' said Caven coldly. He left the airlock.

The two other men on Dervish's team came through the airlock and all three followed Caven back into the ship. The airlock closed behind them.

The space-walk team propelled themselves back to the ship with their jet-packs and entered the ship's forward airlock. Minutes later the black dart of the spaceship detached itself from the beacon streaked away into deep space. Nothing happened for a minute longer. Then the charges detonated in a series of silent explosions.

The beacon disintegrated.

Not far away, another ship was approaching. It was a massive T-shaped vessel – a six-decker bearing the 'striking eagle' insignia of the Space Corps.

It was one of the Space Corps' latest V-ships, an immensely powerful battle-cruiser. Its six decks held laboratories, barracks, repair shops, a hospital and recreation areas. The battle-cruiser was like a city in space, designed for long spells patrolling the outer reaches of Earth's empire.

The cruiser's enormous flight deck was in two tiers. Teams of technicians monitored row upon row of complex instrument banks on the lower level. But on the upper level, the bridge, there was only a single command chair. It was occupied by a man in the white uniform of a general of the Space Corps.

General Nikolai Hermack was a grim-faced man in his early fifties. His close-cropped hair was iron

3

grey, but he was as lean and hard as a man half his age.

Life was a simple matter to General Hermack: a man did his duty at all times and whatever the cost; there was no more to be said.

A tall, pleasant-looking man entered the bridge, saluted and stood waiting. Ian Warne was a high-flyer in every sense of the word. He was a brilliant fighter pilot and one of the youngest majors in the Space Corps. Just as tough as Hermack in his own way, he was more flexible than the older man and something of a diplomat when necessary, which was quite often in his position as General Hermack's aide.

Hermack looked up. 'Any more information on that beacon signal?'

'No, sir. It seems to have just packed up. There's no response on the secondary emergency circuits either.'

'No, there wouldn't be,' said Hermack enigmatically. 'What do you think has happened to that beacon, Major Warne?'

'Difficult to say, sir. It could be a failure in the solar energy storage circuits.'

'No. The emergency power circuits would cut in, and we'd get a mayday signal.'

Warne looked thoughtfully at his superior. 'I gather you don't think this is a mechanical failure, sir?'

'Those beacons are virtually foolproof,' Hermack fell silent for a moment. Then he struck the arm of his command chair with his fist. 'I must be right – I must!'

'Sir?'

4

'Those beacons are constructed almost entirely of argonite, Ian. Nothing else will stand the stresses of long spells in deep space.' Hermack brooded for a moment before leaning forward to flip a switch.

'Attention all personnel. This is General Hermack. This V-ship is now fifty days and as many billions of miles away from Earth.'

All over the ship, men and women stopped what they were doing to listen.

The strong confident voice went on. 'We are now entering the fourth sector of our galaxy. For some time now, Earth Government has been aware that an organized gang of criminals – space pirates if you will – has been preying on defenceless cargo ships. Their main target has always been argonite, the most valuable mineral in the galaxy, found only in the planets of the fourth sector.

'A Government space-beacon marking the approach to the planet of New Sarum has recently ceased transmitting its navigation signals.' Hermack paused impressively. 'As you know, such beacons are constructed largely of argonite. It is my belief that the criminals have now turned to a new source of this precious metal. They have begun attacking the beacons and plundering their argonite.

'In my view there can be no other explanation for the beacon's failure. I have therefore decided to deviate from our scheduled course to investigate the failure of the New Sarum beacon. I will see all section commanders on the bridge at twenty hundred hours.'

No doubt about it, the old boy was impressive, thought Warne. Hermack had deduced a whole new pattern of criminal activity from one non-functioning space-beacon, and he wasn't afraid to back his conclusions with action. Perhaps that was why he was a general.

Warne turned to the star chart on the screen behind the command chair. 'There are eighteen space beacons in this sector, sir.'

'Seventeen, Ian, until New Sarum is replaced.'

'Seventeen, then, sir – all millions of miles apart. How can we tell which one the pirates will choose next?'

Hermack rose and joined him at the star chart. 'We can't.'

'Exactly so, sir. The odds are seventeen to one against our being in the right place at the right time.'

'Then we'll just have to rely on our speed to shorten the odds a bit.' Hermack jabbed a finger at the map. 'There are four beacons grouped fairly close together in the Pliny solar system. That's where we'll start our patrol.'

Beacon Alpha Seven looked identical to the now defunct Alpha One, and it was currently the scene of exactly the same series of events.

A slim, black, dart-shaped ship locked on to the beacon's air-lock. Teams of space-suited men emerged and began busying themselves about the inside and outside of the beacon.

Caven watched impatiently inside the beacon's airlock as Dervish waited to see his team through the airlock. 'Come on, speed it up.'

'I don't like it,' said Dervish gloomily. 'Hitting another beacon so soon.'

'I'm not asking you to like it. Just get those scissor-charges in position.'

'We'll bring the whole darn Space Corps down on us if we go on attacking beacons at this rate.'

Caven shook his head. 'Right now the Space Corps has got trouble on its hands all over the galaxy – little wars in dozens of different sectors. There's never been a better time for getting rich.'

Dervish opened the hatch and beckoned his team into the airlock. 'All right, boys, same procedure as before. We'll place four shots along the main axle and attach repeaters around the hull.'

'You're a good engineer, Dervish,' said Caven patronizingly. 'Just look after your side of the job and leave me to worry about the Space Corps.'

'I spent ten years working for Earth Government,' began Dervish.

'You shouldn't have got sticky fingers, should you?' sneered Caven. 'You could have stayed with it. You'd have got a pension – eventually!'

'Attacking Government property is the one crime they make sure *never* pays.'

Caven slapped the metal bulkhead with a space-gauntleted hand. 'Sixteen tons of pure argonite will pay all right. This isn't just a beacon to me, Dervish – it's a floating bank-roll!'

Warne moved along the lower flight deck of the massive V-ship on a routine inspection. He paused behind the space radar console. 'What range are the forward scanners set for, Penn?'

'Fifteen hundred, sir.'

'Reset them for two thousand.'

'Very good, sir.'

'Keep a good eye on the screens. There are a lot of rogue asteroids in the Pliny system.'

Warne went up to the bridge.

Hermack was barking orders into a communicator. 'Make sure the minnow-ships are fully fuelled and on constant standby, and arm their missiles.'

'We're approaching the Pliny section now, general,' reported Warne. 'We've made routine scanner contact with all four beacons; they're functioning normally.'

Hermack swung round to study the star chart and pointed at it. 'There's Ta, main inhabited planet of the system. We'll orbit it for a few weeks and see what happens.'

'So that's Ta,' said Warne thoughtfully. 'Richest argonite deposits in the galaxy and headquarters of the Issigri Mining Corporation.'

Hermack nodded. 'They say Madeleine Issigri's built quite a city there. It'll be handy for rest and recreation if we're out here long.'

Penn's voice came up from the flight deck. 'Contact on space radar, sir. A spaceship seems to be locked on to Beacon Alpha Seven.'

Warne hurried down to the space radar screen; Hermack followed close behind him.

'Keep locked on to it, Penn,' ordered Warne. 'Any identification?'

'Not yet, sir. Too far away.'

Hermack peered at the screen. 'It's a ship, right enough. Ian, check flight information and see if anything's due out there.'

Hermack grabbed the nearest communicator microphone. 'This is the bridge. Set a course for

8

Beacon Alpha Seven.' He put down the microphone and then snatched it up again. 'Bridge to power room. Give me ten seconds main boost.'

Warne looked up from a screen of data. 'According to flight information there are no ships due at this beacon for the next seventeen days.'

Hermack stared unwinkingly at the blip on the screen. 'So, whoever they are, they haven't logged their flight with Central Flight Information.'

'Do you think it's the pirates, sir?'

'It could be. Mind you, certain commercial flights don't always like to report their precise whereabouts, for reasons of their own. We'll know soon enough.'

'Sir, the ship's leaving the beacon,' called Penn. 'She's backing off.'

'Keep track of her!'

'Doing my best sir – but she's moving away fast.'

Warne studied the fast-moving blip on the screen. 'That's quite a turn of speed for a commercial ship.'

A sudden thought struck Hermack. 'Is Beacon Alpha Seven still functioning normally?'

Penn checked his instruments. 'Yes sir. Signal's loud and clear.'

'Put it on audio.'

Penn obeyed. A steady high-pitched warble filled the flight deck. Suddenly a high-pitched bleeping mingled with the warble of the beacon signal.

'There's another signal coming through as well, sir. It sounds like UHF . . .'

Both signals cut out at once.

Penn looked up from the space radar screen, his face appalled. 'Alpha Seven's broken up, sir.'

9

Hermack's fist smashed down on the nearest console. 'The pirates! They've done it again – and this time right under our noses!'

2

The Intruders

'We've lost the beacon, sir,' reported Penn. 'No radar trace, and no more signal.'

'There won't be,' said Warne grimly. 'By now that beacon's in a dozen separate pieces.'

Hermack was glaring angrily at the moving blip on the screen. 'Penn! Make sure you hold the contact with that pirate ship! At least we can make sure they don't get away. Major Warne, give me a projected arrival time.'

Warne punched buttons on a computer console. 'Three hours, sir.' He turned to a nearby technician. 'See if you can get a visual of them on the long-range scanner.'

Moments later the black dart-shaped pirate vessel came into focus on the scanner. It seemed to be trailed by a scattering of squared-off shapes.

'There she is, sir,' said Warne. 'And there's what's left of the beacon!'

'Then we've got them cold,' said Hermack with savage satisfaction. 'We'll be up with them long before they can salvage the argonite from the beacon.'

'As long as they don't spot us approaching, sir. That ship looks fast.'

'They don't even know we're in the area,' said Hermack confidently.

'The ship's moving away now, sir,' said Penn. 'She's just increased speed. Sir, the debris is moving too!'

'Penn, *keep that contact*,' ordered Hermack.

Penn's hands were busy at the console. 'It's no use, sir, she's going faster and moving right out of range.'

Hermack glared at the screen in frustrated rage. 'She must have at least twice our speed!'

'The minnow-ships could hold her,' suggested Warne.

'Not at this distance, not for long. They simply don't have the range.'

Penn looked up from his screen. 'Contact lost, sir.'

Warne turned away in despair. 'They must have attached rocket propulsion units to the sections of beacon, sir.'

'Oh yes, they're very well organized,' said Hermack disgustedly. 'They cut the beacon into manageable sections and shoot the bits off to some prearranged collection point. Very clever!'

'And quicker too,' Warne pointed out. 'Cuts down the time they're at risk. They can burn out the argonite at leisure.'

Hermack was pacing up and down the flight

deck. 'We've got to rethink our tactics, Ian. We'll never catch them by normal patrol methods.'

Warne looked puzzled. 'What else *can* we do sir?'

Hermack demonstrated the talent for cutting to the heart of a problem that made him a general. 'Man the beacons! It's the only answer. We'll drop small parties of four or five men at every beacon in the sector. We'll leave them supplies for two months.'

Warne looked stunned. 'I know the beacons are meant to serve as emergency survival stations, but I don't think anyone's ever tried living on them, sir.'

'The men may not be very comfortable, but they'll survive,' said Hermack ruthlessly. 'Set course for the nearest beacon!'

Some hours later, the massive V-ship was docked beside Beacon Alpha Four, and Major Warne was installing Lieutenant Sorba and a party of four Space Corps guardsmen on board the beacon.

He handed Sorba a small black box. 'Here's your emergency signal, lieutenant. It will beam out automatically to main control. Remember, your purpose here is to give us the earliest possible warning of an approaching pirate. The first sign of trouble, you press the switch, OK?'

Sorba, a lean, dark-featured man said: 'I'll press it, sir, don't worry.' He gave a wolfish grin. 'After that can we fight?'

'After that, Joe, you'll probably have to! Good luck!'

Sorba saluted smartly. 'Thank you, sir.'

Returning the salute, Warne went back through

13

the airlock. The V-ship drew away from the beacon a few minutes later.

'Set a course for Beacon Alpha Nine,' ordered Hermack.

Warne entered the flight deck and saluted. 'Beacon party installed, sir. I told Lieutenant Sorba we'd be back in about six weeks.'

'We'll be back much earlier if the pirates raid Alpha Four. How is morale?'

'Pretty high, sir. I think Joe's looking forward to a fight.'

'They understand they're to shoot on sight?'

'Don't worry, sir. Anyone poking his nose aboard Alpha Four will probably get it blown off!'

The silence of the computer bay of Beacon Alpha Four was shattered by a strange wheezing, groaning sound. The incongruous shape of a square blue police box materialized in the corner of the instrument-filled room.

Alpha Four, like all the other beacons, was a honeycomb of different-sized compartments, most of them packed with instruments. Others held stores and equipment, and one or two had been left empty to provide the most basic of living accommodation, intended only for emergency use.

The compartments were linked by ladders, hatches and companionways leading to a variety of metal corridors.

One of the guards, young, inexperienced and very excited, clattered down a metal ladder and rushed up to Lieutenant Sorba who was briefing the other guards.

'Sir!' he gasped.

Sorba swung round. 'What is it? Why aren't you at your post in the observation dome.'

'There's something in the computer bay, sir!'

'What sort of something?'

'Don't know, sir. I was passing it on my way to the observation dome when I heard something in there – a strange noise.'

Sorba looked sceptically at the young guard, wondering if he was listening to the effects of an overheated imagination. 'All right, I suppose we'd better check it out.'

The door of the police box opened and a strangely assorted trio emerged.

First came a rather scruffy little man in baggy chequered trousers and an ill-fitting frock coat, which he wore with a wide-collared white shirt and a straggly bow tie. His deeply-lined face, wise, gentle and funny all at once, was surmounted by a mop of untidy black hair. Known only as the Doctor, he was a Time Lord, a wanderer through space and time.

He was followed by a brawny, truculent young man in the kilt of a Scottish Highlander. His name was James Robert McCrimmon – Jamie for short – and he had been snatched from the eighteenth century to join the Doctor in his wanderings.

Then came a small, pretty dark-haired girl in neatly tailored shorts and a crisp white jacket and blouse. She was called Zoe Herriot. Before joining the Doctor she had been a computer operator on a space station – in some ways she was a bit of a human computer herself.

The Doctor looked round the little room. 'Oh dear!'

'What's wrong?' asked Zoe suspiciously.

'I don't think we're quite where I expected. Never mind, this looks very interesting.'

Jamie sniffed. 'Interesting? It's just a lot of old machinery.'

'Exactly, Jamie. I don't think I've ever seen computers quite like this before.'

Zoe looked round. 'It's some kind of control room, isn't it Doctor?'

'Yes, but what is it controlling?'

Zoe didn't know.

Jamie didn't want to know. 'If you ask me, we should get out of here right away.'

Zoe pointed. 'There's a door over there.'

'I dinna mean we should go wandering off. I mean we should leave in the TARDIS before someone turns up and starts asking questions.'

'Don't worry, Jamie,' said the Doctor. 'I can assure you there's nobody here to bother us.'

'What makes you so sure?'

The Doctor pointed to the instrument-lined walls. 'All these devices are designed to operate by themselves.'

'But what do they do, Doctor?' asked Zoe. 'Where are we?'

'On an unmanned spacecraft in a fixed orbit, I should imagine. Let's see if we can find some more clues as to its purpose, shall we?'

The Doctor opened the hatch Zoe had indicated, and he and Zoe climbed through.

16

Jamie was just about to follow them when he heard a sudden clatter of booted feet on metal. It seemed to be coming from underneath him.

He paused in the hatchway listening.

Suddenly a circular hatch in the middle of the floor was flung open. A uniformed figure appeared, clutching a blaster.

Jamie might have a problem with technology, but there was nothing wrong with his reflexes.

He flung himself through the open hatchway just as a bolt from a blaster ricocheted off its edge.

Slamming shut the hatch behind him, Jamie yelled: 'Look out!' and dashed down the corridor to where the Doctor and Zoe were waiting. He heard more muffled shots echoing through the hatch.

'Nobody here, eh?' said Jamie bitterly.

Zoe looked at the Doctor. 'Now what are we going to do? The TARDIS is back there – where they're shooting at us!'

The shots grew louder and nearer. The hatch opened and a blaster-bolt sizzled down the corridor.

'There's only one thing we can do,' said the Doctor. 'Run!'

He set off down the corridor with Jamie and Zoe close behind him.

'Next time you'll mebbe listen to me,' said Jamie.

'If there is a next time,' said Zoe.

In the computer bay, the baffled Lieutenant Sorba was staring at the TARDIS. 'They must have smuggled themselves on board in this thing. They were here, waiting for us all the time!'

He turned to his men. 'All right, there are only

three of them and they can't get away. Hunt them down, and don't forget your orders: shoot to kill!'

In the excitement of the hunt, Sorba and his men were completely unaware of one very important event. A slim, black, dart-shaped ship was gliding up to the docking bay of Beacon Alpha Four.

3

Trapped

Caven stood looking round the airlock. It felt very familiar, because all the beacons were built to the same design.

'Welcome to Alpha Four,' he said satirically. 'Another present from the taxpayers of our beloved home planet!'

Dervish, worried as ever, didn't raise a smile. 'Same procedure as last time?'

Caven slapped him on the back. 'That's right, Dervish!' His voice hardened. 'Now you've had a bit of practice, get those scissor-charges laid a bit quicker, will you?'

Suddenly they heard the muffled thump of blaster fire from somewhere inside the beacon. Dervish was stunned, but Caven reacted with his usual brisk efficiency. 'Get the crew in here – on the double!'

The Doctor, Jamie and Zoe pounded along another corridor, then climbed up a ladder and through a hatchway into the corridor above.

The Doctor threw a locking bar across the hatch. 'There – that'll hold them for a while.'

'Are you all right, Zoe?' asked Jamie chivalrously.

Zoe was more indignant than frightened. 'We haven't done anything. Why are they trying to kill us, Doctor?'

'I don't know, but we can't stop to find out!'

Jamie sniffed. 'Doctor, look!'

A wisp of smoke was rising from the hatch below them. Suddenly a fiery line began moving along the hatch-cover.

'Come along,' said the Doctor briskly. 'I think we'd better find somewhere to hide!'

They made their way through several more doors and hatches – and found themselves in an empty metal chamber. The only entrance was the doorway by which they'd entered.

'It's a dead end,' said Zoe. 'Now what do we do?'

She turned to go back, but the Doctor put out a hand to prevent her. 'I don't know, Zoe. If we go back into that passage we'll walk straight into them. We're trapped!'

Lieutenant Sorba and his men were using focused blaster beams to burn through the last of the hatches that separated them from the intruders.

Sorba broke down the hatch with a couple of hefty kicks; the charred hatch-cover clanged to the floor. He was about to burst through when he heard the crackle of blaster-fire behind him.

He swung round to see a motley group of space-suited figures shooting down his men.

Sorba swung up his blaster to fire, but a bolt from the blaster of one of the attackers took him in the right shoulder and his weapon spun from his hand.

Wounded as he was, Lieutenant Sorba knew his duty. With his left hand he snatched convulsively at the signal radio in his belt. His thumb came down on the transmit button just as blackness flooded over him.

'Thirty minutes to Beacon Alpha Three,' reported Penn.

Hermack nodded, still staring at the star-chart. 'Right! Beacon party on standby, Ian.'

Warne had already started to move away when a low warbling came from the long-range communications console.

'Emergency on Beacon Alpha Four, sir!' shouted Penn.

Warne swung round. 'Sorba must be under attack!'

'Set a course for Alpha Four,' snapped Hermack. He grabbed the communications microphone. 'Bridge to power room. I want maximum boost – for as long as you can hold it without vaporizing the engines!'

Caven rolled over the prostrate Sorba with his foot; the lieutenant moaned and stirred.

'Looks like this one's still alive.'

Dervish wasn't used to bloodshed and he was close to panic. 'So the Space Corps are too busy to bother about us, are they?'

'Shut up, Dervish, I'm thinking.'

'Too late for thinking, we've got to get out of here.'

Caven looked thoughtfully along the body-littered corridor. 'Four Space Corps guardsmen and an officer . . . What were they doing here?'

'There must be a battle-cruiser in the area,' said Dervish worriedly. 'I warned you.'

Ignoring him, Caven pursued his train of thought. 'Not a big enough party to defend the beacon against an attack in force, but they must have been put aboard for some reason . . .' He bent to look at the device in Sorba's hand, prising it loose from the unconscious man's fingers. 'Now then, what have we here?'

Dervish examined the device. 'It looks like a fixed beam transmitter of some kind.' He looked up in alarm. 'That's it, Caven, that's what they've done. Their ship will be on its way back here right now!'

'Then we'd better get moving,' said Caven calmly. 'I take it the charges are all in place?'

'Well, very nearly but . . .' Dervish stared at him, 'you're not still going to blow up the beacon?'

'That's what we came here for, isn't it? So let's not waste any more time, Dervish. Get on with it!'

Caven threw the transmitter to the floor, raised his blaster and blew it to bits.

On the flight deck of the battle-cruiser the warbling of the signalling device cut out. For a moment no one spoke.

Warne said tentatively: 'Could be just that their radio's packed up sir.'

'Yes. Projected arrival time, Penn?'

'Two hours, twenty minutes, sir.'

Hermack's voice was unusually subdued. 'I should have left Sorba more men.'

'The beacon couldn't hold a force of any size, sir,' said Warne steadily. 'Sorba and his men were all volunteers. They knew they could hope only to delay things.'

General Hermack's voice was a low, murderous growl. 'I'm going to get that gang of murdering thieves if it's the last thing I do.'

Sorba stirred and struggled to sit up, clutching his wounded shoulder. He looked along the corridor at the slumped, lifeless bodies of his men.

A dark thin-faced man stood looking down at him, covering him with a blaster.

Caven smiled coldly, 'Yes, lieutenant, they're all dead – I checked. I'm afraid you're the last of the tin soldiers.'

'Shot in the back,' said Sorba bitterly.

'Does that mean we're disqualified, lieutenant? You don't want to play any more?'

'You won't get away with this,' said Sorba feebly.

'No? Who's going to stop me, lieutenant?'

Sorba struggled to remember recent events. 'How did you get those decoys on board?'

Caven was genuinely puzzled. 'What decoys?'

'The three who lead us into your ambush.'

Caven stared at him. 'Suffering from concussion, lieutenant, or just stalling for time?'

'You know what I'm talking about. They ran through into the aft companionway.'

'Come to think of it, we did hear firing down here. You mean there really is someone else on board?'

'We thought you'd planted them.'

Caven shook his head. 'None of my men down here. Well, whoever they are, I've no time to worry about them.'

Dervish came hurrying down the corridor. 'All the charges are laid. They're just fixing the last of the rockets now.'

Caven nodded towards Sorba. 'If he can walk, get him out of here. If not, leave him.' He aimed his blaster at the hatchway, fusing its edges into a mass of molten metal.

Dervish looked at him in amazement. 'What are you doing?'

'Sealing a coffin,' said Caven. 'Now come on, let's get moving!'

Inside the little metal room, the Doctor and his companions stared at the smoking door.

'Are they trying to burn through it, Doctor?' asked Zoe.

'I don't know, Zoe.' The Doctor was listening at the door. 'It sounds as if they're going away . . .' He tried the door, and snatched his fingers away. 'It's still hot.' There was a booming clanging sound. 'Now it sounds as if someone's moving on the hull.'

'What do you think they're doing, Doctor?' asked Jamie.

'Cleaning the windows?'

24

Jamie groaned.

'Why don't we sneak back to the TARDIS and get out of here?' suggested Zoe.

'A sensible suggestion,' said the Doctor solemnly, 'just so long as there's no one out there, Zoe!'

Zoe had her ear to the hatch. 'I haven't heard a sound for ages. Come on!'

She grabbed the locking wheel and tried to turn it. It refused to move.

Jamie edged her aside. 'You need to eat more porridge, girl. Let me try.' Jamie heaved until his muscles cracked, but the wheel refused to budge.

The Doctor came to join him and together they struggled with the wheel. It was still no use.

Suddenly the Doctor understood. 'We might as well give up, Jamie. They've welded the lock!'

Zoe frowned. 'Why would they do that?'

'To keep us in here, obviously. We seem to be prisoners.'

Hermack and Warne were grouped around Penn's radar screen.

'The ship's leaving the beacon, sir,' reported Penn.

Warne nodded. 'It's exactly like it was before,'

'What's our arrival time, Penn?' growled Hermack.

'Ninety minutes, sir.'

'We're going to be too late again!' Hermack said bitterly

'If they're following the same procedure,' said Warne 'that beacon will blow any second now!'

The Doctor and his companions reeled as the little

25

room in which they were imprisoned suddenly twisted and spun.

A dense cloud of smoke poured into the room and they fell back choking . . .

4

The Renegade

Technician Penn stared intently at the space radar screen, uncomfortably aware that General Hermack was leaning over his shoulder.

'Give me a bearing on that pirate ship, Penn,' ordered Hermack.

Penn stared desperately at the screen. 'Can't pick her up, sir.'

'*What?*'

'I can't pick her up, sir. The debris of the beacon is jamming the signals.'

'Penn, you incompetent, useless piece of space-flotsam . . .' With a sort of a choked-off growl, Hermack turned and strode away.

Major Warne, who had been hovering discreetly in the background, gave Penn a consolatory tap on the shoulder. 'Just keep trying, Penn. Carry on.'

'Yes sir,' said Penn gratefully, and resumed his study of the screen.

Warne moved to the far end of the bridge to join Hermack. The general was standing by a refreshment station watching black coffee trickle into a plastic cup.

He glared evilly at Warne. 'Coffee?'

Hermack punched the appropriate buttons without waiting for a reply and handed the cup to Warne.

'Thank you, sir,' said Warne stiffly.

For a few moments the two men stood sipping the bitter coffee in silence.

Then Hermack growled: 'All right, all right, I know. The men are doing their best, and Penn's the best radar-technician in the fleet.'

Warne gave him a look of innocent enquiry. 'General?'

'Isn't that what you were going to say?'

'Something like that, sir.'

Hermack turned and moved back to the space radar screen. 'You see? Now even the debris is moving out of range.'

'If we could sustain continuous main boost it might be a different story,' said Warne ruefully. 'We're fifty days out from home planet, and they've probably got a base somewhere in this system.'

Hermack nodded. 'Quite, so they can use main boost all the time. Our only chance will be to get close enough to launch the minnow-ships.'

'Or locate their base, sir. The bits of that beacon must have been dispatched there. If we could track down one of the segments . . .'

Hermack shook his head. 'Can't be done. Once those auxiliary rockets cut out, there's no energy-source to track.' He gestured towards the screen. 'You see – nothing there now!'

'We could try the tactile scanner, general.'

The tactile scanner sensed the presence of solid bodies in space, but it would work only for objects considerably larger than a few segments of space beacon.

'It would be like looking for a single speck of dust at the bottom of an argonite mine,' said Hermack dismissively, and turned away.

Warne remained staring at the screen. 'Do you think there's any chance they might still be alive?'

Hermack swung round. 'Lieutenant Sorba and his men? I doubt it, major. I very much doubt if there's anyone still alive on that beacon by now.'

But General Hermack was wrong. A little air still remained in one of the sealed beacon segments that drifted purposefully through space.

Inside, the Doctor, Jamie and Zoe were just beginning to stir.

Relieved to have something to report at last, Penn looked up from his screen. 'Major Warne!'

Warne hurried over. 'What is it?'

'Rocket ship, sir.'

'Are you sure?'

'No doubt about it, sir. She's right in the area I've been scanning – where Alpha Four went up!'

'Can you get me a visual scan?'

'Should be able to, sir.' Pen swung round to a nearby console. 'Bearing starboard nineteen.'

Hermack hurried over. 'Something happened?'

'Penn's just picked up something on radar, general.'

'One of the pirates?'

'If it is them, they're acting very oddly, sir. That ship's hardly moving.'

'Maybe they haven't realized we're in the area.'

'The pirates must know there's a V-ship in the area,' Warne pointed out.' They've just run into our party on Alpha Four. Somehow, I don't think this can be them. They're hardly likely to be loitering near the scene of the crime.'

Hermack was suspicious by nature. 'According to flight information, *nothing* is due in this area for the next eighty hours.'

On a nearby screen, the shape of a rocket ship started to become clear.

'There she is!' said Warne. 'I'm afraid it isn't the ship we caught sight of before, general.'

'No, it isn't. Try to get a closer shot, Penn.'

Penn punched controls, and the image on the screen grew larger. It showed a battered, stubby, curiously old-fashioned rocket ship.

Its battered hull was dented and pitted by numerous meteor-scars and it bore the insignia LIZ 79, painted in sprawling letters on the clumsy nose-cone.

Warne stared at it in disbelief. 'That's one of the old Delta class freighters, sir. I didn't know there were any of them left in space.'

Inside the battered old spaceship that was causing General Hermack and Major Warne so much concern, an equally battered old space pilot was about to start breakfast.

Milo Clancey was a stocky, heavily-moustached man in his early sixties, as tough and weather-beaten as his ship. He sat now in the pilot's chair of its stark metallic flight cabin, surrounded by old-fashioned patched-up controls.

He wore the trousers to an old-fashioned heavy-duty space-suit – the tunic was draped over the back of his chair – together with a garish tartan shirt and a gaudy neck-scarf.

He was staring expectantly at a slot in his control console. The slot gave out a sudden puff of steam and a boiled egg rolled into the container below.

Scooping up the egg, Milo popped it into the egg-cup which stood with a coffee pot and mug on a nearby tray. Drawing a formidable-looking knife from its belt-sheath, Milo lopped off the top of the egg. He then stared expectantly at a smoking metal container on top of the console.

The hinged lid of the container suddenly snapped back. Two blackened objects that had once been slices of toast shot out.

Milo looked at them in disgust, and then hurled bread and toaster across the cabin. 'The last of me bread! Stupid new-fangled solar toasters!'

Above his head an illumintated panel bearing the word 'CALL' began flickering feebly.

Milo flicked a switch, and a speaker gave out a roar of static. He twiddled a knob and a voice emerged through the crackle.

'This is V–41 calling calling LIZ 79. V–41 calling LIZ 79. Can you hear me?'

Milo flicked another switch, shoved a spoonful of egg in his mouth and said indistinctly: 'I hear you V–41. Go away!'

There was another sputter of static and the voice said: 'This is General Nikolai Hermack of the Space Fleet, First Division. Give me your identity reading.'

Milo took a swig of coffee. 'Oh, take yourself off will you now, general? I'm having me breakfast!'

He dug out another spoonful of egg.

On the flight deck of the battle-cruiser, Technician Penn and Major Warne were almost painfully straight-faced, neither daring to catch the other's eye.

General Hermack on the other hand was slowly turning an alarming shade of purple.

As Major Warne hurried to a computer terminal, Hermack snarled: 'LIZ 79, give me your identity registration code. That is an order.'

'General, I forgot all that rigmarole years ago,' said the voice from the speaker. 'Now be a good laddie and away about your business!'

Just in time to avert an explosion, Major Warne hurried up with a computer print-out. 'LIZ 79's registration, sir. She's a real antique – been in service more than forty years.'

Hermack looked at the information sheet. 'Milo Clancey! I might have known,'

'You know him, sir?'

'I know *of* him. Out in Reja Magnum, where I did my first tour, he was a bit of a legend.' Hermack turned back to the communicator microphone. 'Milo Clancey! I have your identity registration here.'

'Well, isn't that fine now general. You'll be happy now, will you? Good day to you!'

'Now you listen to me, Clancey! Where are you from and where are you bound?'

'And what possible business would that be of yours?' demanded the voice indignantly.

Hermack's patience snapped. 'Clancey, I'm coming alongside and locking on. I'm sending a patrol to bring you aboard for interrogation. I warn you, don't try to resist.

On board LIZ 79, Milo Clancey shrugged philosophically. 'Suit yourself, general. Mind you don't scratch your lovely new paint now!'

At the end of the day, thought Milo, the big boys could make you do as they said. But they couldn't make you like it.

5

The Survivors

On board the now detached main segment of Beacon Alpha Four, the Doctor suddenly rolled over and sat up, clutching his aching head. He looked at his two motionless companions and shook them gently in turn, attempting to rouse them.

'Jamie, come on now. Zoe, wake up!'

Neither of them moved.

Looking round the crampled cabin the Doctor saw an oxygen cylinder clamped to the wall.

Struggling to his feet he unhooked it and carried it over to his unconscious, playing the stream of oxygen over their faces.

They began to stir.

Major Warne saluted. 'They're bringing Clancey on board now, sir. Apparently he didn't give any trouble.'

'He won't co-operate though,' said General

35

Hermack gloomily. 'Ever run across any of these old-timers, Ian?'

'Not really, sir.'

'They think they're a law unto themselves – and they don't like the Space Corps one bit.'

'Why not, sir?'

Hermack stared reminiscently into space, remembering his days as a young lieutenant. 'People like Clancey – miners and prospectors – were the first men to go out into deep space. For a long time they had it to themselves. They went wherever they wanted, fought over mineral rights, jumped each other's claims. They were a wild lot, and they got used to living without rules.'

'And then the Space Corps came along and started enforcing law and order?'

Hermack nodded. 'Exactly – much to their resentment. Milo Clancey must be one of the last of the breed.'

As if to prove his words, Milo Clancey shambled on to the bridge under the escort of a couple of nervous young troopers.

Clancey had made no attempt to dress for the occasion. He still wore his ancient space-suit trousers and tartan shirt. The only addition was an old but still serviceable blaster rifle resting casually over one shoulder. So far no one had felt like trying to take it away from him.

Milo Clancey looked round the gleaming bridge with exaggerated, wide-eyed admiration. 'They certainly do you Space Corps slickers proud – it's a whole flying fun-palace you have here!'

Hermack decided it was time to take control of the interview.

36

'Milo Clancey?' he boomed. 'I am General Hermack, this is Major Warne, my aide. I shall come straight to the point. I want to know what you're doing in this system, and why you are not on feedback to Central Flight Information.'

Milo Clancey sighed. 'To be honest with you, general, my feedback circuit burned out about five years ago – or was it ten? I've been meaning to get it fixed.'

Major Warne was shocked. 'Surely you must know it's an offence to operate without proper feedback to CFI?'

'An offence, is it? Oh dear! There are so many offences these days, aren't there?'

Hermack said sternly: 'And what is your business in this sector, Clancey?'

'Well, you see now, I'm the head of the Clancey Space Mining Company.'

Hermack brandished the print-out. 'We know that, it's all here on your file.'

'Sure, and what a wonderful thing it is to have all those facts at your fingertips, general.'

'Just get to the point, man.'

Milo Clancey's voice hardened. 'You'd know the point, general, if anyone had been taking any notice of the reports I've been sending for the last two years.'

'Reports? What about?' snapped Warne.

'About argonite pirates, sonny. In the past two years I've lost five floaters carrying argonite ore back to Earth. They were hijacked and brought somewhere in this system.'

'You say you've reported this?'

'A dozen times – and a fat lot of notice anyone's

37

taken. So I thought, right, I'll have to do something myself!'

'How much argonite did you have on each floater?' demanded Hermack.

'About fifty thousand tons of unrefined ore. It's not economic to send less.'

'What makes you so sure the stolen floaters were taken somewhere in this system?' asked Warne curiously.

'Time, sonny. This is the nearest system to the point where they vanished from the spaceways. Floaters are unmanned with no propulsion units – they don't move very fast . . .' Clancey broke off, sneezing. 'Is it all right if I blow my nose, sonny, or is that an offence too?'

Without waiting for a reply Clancey produced a grubby handkerchief and blew a resounding blast.

'My poor old nose just isn't used to this fancy air-conditioning.'

Hermack tried to get the interrogation back on course. 'How long have you been in the vicinity of Beacon Alpha Four?'

Milo Clancey scratched his head. 'Beacon Alpha Four? Now where might that be, general?'

Hermack jabbed a finger at the star chart on a nearby screen. 'Here!'

Clancey peered at the screen. 'Sure, there's nothing there, general. I tell you those beacons just aren't reliable – a waste of public money if you ask me.'

'Alpha Four isn't registering on the chart, Clancey, because it isn't there any more. It was blown into segments by argonite pirates and taken away.'

'Is that so?' said Milo Clancey softly. 'For salvage you mean? Aye, that would be it . . .'

He seemed lost in thought.

'You don't seem very surprised, Clancey,' said General Hermack coldly.

'I'm not, general. That explains what you're doing here. I can lose every floater I've got and your fancy Space Corps couldn't care less. But one government beacon goes missing and that's a different story, eh?'

'When we've caught these pirates,' said Hermack pompously, 'and if your story can be proved, then you'll be entitled to put in a claim for compensation.'

'When and if,' scoffed Clancey. 'If I wait until you catch them, I'll be waiting for ever. That marauding bunch of sharks have a Beta Dart, one of the latest ships, and with about twice your speed! You might just as well turn round and go home.'

Warne looked at him with sudden suspicion. 'How do you know what type of ship they're using?'

'Because I crossed their thieving flight path a couple of times, sonny, when I was being robbed! If my old LIZ had the speed I'd have rammed them!'

The Doctor was standing on Jamie's broad shoulders and peering through a small observation port set high in the wall. In the distance he could see other segments of the beacon, floating in a silent, eerie convoy.

'All right, Jamie, let me down now.'

The Doctor clambered down and Jamie said eagerly: 'What's on the other side? Could you see?'

'I'm afraid there's nothing on the other side. Just space.'

Zoe looked at the sealed hatchway below the window. 'But we just came through there!'

'We did indeed, Zoe, but that was before this machine we're travelling in was blown into several pieces.'

Zoe nodded calmly. 'That must have been the explosion that knocked us out!'

Jamie was still baffled, but his practical mind went straight to the main problem. 'Does that mean we've lost the TARDIS, Doctor?'

'Yes, Jamie.'

'Why would anyone want to blow up this thing?' asked Zoe.

The Doctor shrugged. 'Sabotage, perhaps.'

'What about those men who fired at us?'

'I rather think they were here to defend this place. They must have thought *we* were the attackers, that's why they were so unfriendly.

'So we've landed in the middle of some kind of space war,' said Jamie grimly.

'And now we're stuck on a chunk of space debris,' said Zoe gloomily.' Just drifting aimlessly.'

'Not aimlessly, Zoe,' corrected the Doctor. 'The other pieces of the machine seem to have rockets attached to them. They're all moving in the same direction at the same speed, keeping about a mile apart.'

'So, whoever broke up the machine is sending all the pieces to the same place?'

Jamie's mind was still preoccupied with his main concern. 'So mebbe we can get back to the

TARDIS after all, Doctor? If it's only a mile away . . .'

'A mile in space,' said the Doctor gently. 'Without oxygen or any means of propulsion?'

'It might be as well be a thousand miles,' said Zoe.

Jamie gave them both a disgusted look. 'Och, that's just fine!'

The Doctor suddenly pressed his ear to a section of wall. He seemed to be listening intently.

'Got an idea, Doctor?' asked Zoe hopefully.

'Listen,' said the Doctor.

Zoe listened. 'There seems to be a faint buzzing.'

'Exactly,' said the Doctor. 'I wonder what it is?'

General Hermack took Milo Clancey through his story several times without persuading him to change it or add anything new.

Clancey finally lost patience. 'If you've finished asking stupid questions, general, I'd like to get back to my ship.'

To Warne's surprise, Hermack agreed at once. 'Very well, Mr Clancey. I'm sorry to have detained you.'

'You mean I can go?' asked Clancey cautiously.

'Of course. Is there anything you need, by the way – any supplies or anything of that sort?'

All Milo Clancey wanted was to be on his way. 'That's very kind of you, general, but I'm fully equipped.'

'In that case I'll say goodbye.' Hermack beckoned to a waiting trooper. 'See that Mr Clancey is escorted back to his ship.'

'Goodbye then, and thanks,' said Clancey, and hurried away.

Hermack smiled coldly as he watched Clancey go. When the old-timer's shambling figure had left the flight deck, Hermack glanced quickly at Warne, catching his aide's expression of shocked disapproval.

'You obviously think I've done the wrong thing, Ian.'

'That's not for me to say, sir.'

'You think I let Clancey go too easily?'

'I would have questioned him under the mind probe, sir.'

'The thought did occur to me. He seems to be very well informed about these argonite pirates, doesn't he? Do you think he might even be in league with them?'

'I think it's very possible, sir. You said yourself that he hadn't got much respect for the law. Even the story about his stolen argonite floaters could just be a cover.'

'I quite agree,' said Hermack smoothly. 'In my opinion Milo Clancey is the man behind the whole pirate organization – which is precisely why I let him go!'

Warne stared at him for a moment before giving a sudden grin of comprehension. He spun round to the nearest communications microphone. 'Bridge to armoury. This is Major Warne. I want a minnow-ship readied for immediate launch. Fit Martian missiles with contact warheads.'

With the aid of his trusty sonic screwdriver, the

42

Doctor had succeeded in removing an inspection panel.

Jamie yawned. 'What d'you think he's up to now?'

Zoe shrugged. 'No idea. Ask him!'

'Och, it's no use. He's got his mysterious face on.'

'I think he's just trying to keep our hopes up,' said Zoe quietly.

'How do you mean?'

'By looking busy right up to the end,' explained Zoe calmly. 'Really, there's nothing anyone can do now. We've got only a few hours at the outside.'

Jamie stared at her in alarm. 'What do you mean, only a few hours?'

'Haven't you noticed, Jamie? Haven't you noticed how difficult it's getting to breathe?'

6

Pursuit

General Hermack was pacing up and down the flight deck.

'Penn, you're to keep constant track of Major Warne in the minnow. Let me know as soon as he's in visual range of Clancey's ship.'

'Yes, sir,' said Penn patiently.

Hermack took a few more paces to and fro. 'Tell him – never mind, I'll speak to him myself.' He snatched up a communications microphone. 'V-Master to Minnow Twenty-one, come in. Come in Minnow Twenty-one.'

The minnows were light, fast manoeuvrable scout-ships, a sort of deep space equivalent to old-fashioned atmospheric fighter-planes.

Inside the cramped cockpit of the tiny ship, Warne flicked his communicator switch. 'Minnow Twenty-one to V-Master.'

'This is General Hermack. What's your situation?'

'Everything's OK, general. My tracking system's locked on to Clancey's ship, and I'm pretty sure he doesn't know I'm tailing him.'

'Well done, Ian. But remember, Milo Clancey's no fool. If he does suspect you're following him, there'll be trouble. I'm going to visit the Issigri mining headquarters on Ta and see what I can find out there.'

The Doctor lifted the panel clear of the wall to reveal a jumble of power cables and junction boxes. 'Just as I thought – solar powered construction along the lines of its electromagnetic fields.'

Weak as she was, Zoe's scientific mind was intrigued. 'You mean the rocket was built in sections and assembled by magnetism – and the explosion broke the magnetic attraction between each section?'

'Exactly, Zoe! Now, if I can step up the electromagnetic power to bridge the space between this section and the next . . .'

'Draw it towards us, you mean?'

'That's right. We could repeat the process with the next section and the next until we reach the TARDIS!'

Zoe frowned. 'How do you know the next section is an opposite pole? Unlike poles attract, but like poles repel. You might just send the next section shooting off in the opposite direction!'

'Don't be so pessimistic, Zoe,' said the Doctor reproachfully. 'Jamie, just help me to move this hatch cover out of the way will you?'

Undeterred by Zoe's doubts, the Doctor set to work. After all, any plan was better than none.

The head office of the Issigri Mining Corporation on Ta was the most up-to-date and luxurious of all the underground installations on that remote frontier planet. After all, it was the headquarters of one of the richest and most powerful organizations in the galaxy.

Madeleine Issigri, president of the corporation, was fully as impressive as her office. A tall, dark-haired, strikingly beautiful young woman, she had the kind of well-groomed aloof good looks that kept others at a respectful distance. Her manner had the calm authority of someone accustomed to wealth and power.

At the moment she was leaning back in her chair, a faint smile on her lips, watching as General Hermack made free with her company's ultra-modern space communications service.

The screen showed the head and shoulders of the space-suited Major Warne against the background of his tiny instrument-crammed cockpit.

'I'm still maintaining contact with Clancey's ship, general. Nothing more to report.'

The screen went blank.

'It must be *extremely* uncomfortable inside one of those minnow-ships, general,' said Madeleine Issigri, a hint of mockery in her voice.

'It is at first, but you hardly notice it after a week or two.'

She shuddered. 'And may I ask why Milo Clancey is being followed?'

'I suspect him of having some connection with the argonite pirates,' said Hermack bluntly.

'But surely he has his own argonite mines on Lobos.'

'Worked out, I hear.'

Madeleine Issigri smiled. 'That's what they said about my mines on this planet. I brought in up-to-date technology, and now they're the most productive in the galaxy.'

Hermack looked thoughtfully at her. 'Surely you're not defending Clancey – you, of all people? Wasn't he once your father's partner, and didn't he have something to do with your father's mysterious death?'

'I thought so at the time, general, but I could never prove it.'

'And now you run the most successful argonite mines in the galaxy, while Clancey is nearly bankrupt.'

'And you think he's taken to piracy?'

Hermack shrugged. 'For a man like Clancey to find a woman beating him at his own game . . . He might think it was worth any risk to get even.'

'I'd hate to think that was so. He and my father were friends and partners for years.'

'Your concern does you credit, Miss Issigri. In any event we should have proof within the next few hours.'

'How?'

'According to Warne's report, Clancey has been in the same dimensional orbit for quite some time. My theory is that he has a rendezvous with the pirate ship. And if he has . . . I've got him!'

Hermack clenched his hand into a fist.

The Doctor gave Jamie and Zoe a brief blast of oxygen. 'I think that's all we can spare for the moment.'

As far as Jamie could see, the Doctor had simply arranged the tangle of wires and cables into an even greater tangle. 'Will it take much longer, Doctor?' he asked feebly.

'No, no, it's practically ready now. There's just one last connection . . .'

'Aye, well, I just hope it works.'

'Of course it will work, Jamie,' said the Doctor, with an indignant look at Zoe. 'The theory is absolutely sound! Now then, are you ready?'

'Ready, Doctor,' said Zoe.

The Doctor pulled a switch and a low humming noise filled the little cabin. Rising steadily in frequency, it soon turned into an ear-splitting shriek.

The whole cabin started to vibrate.

'You've got it wrong, Doctor,' shouted Zoe. 'We're gathering speed!'

The Doctor tried to pull back the switch but it wouldn't budge. 'The power's too great, I can't shut it off . . .' He looked apologetically at Zoe. 'I'm afraid you were right, my dear. Instead of being attracted we're being repelled – shot out further into space!'

Sprawled in his chair, feet up on the console, Milo Clancey was trusting his beloved LIZ to the care of the automatic pilot. Suddenly a nearby console began giving out an insistent beep.

Milo reached out a foot and kicked it, but the bleeping only became louder.

Yawning, Milo got to his feet and wandered over to another console.

He flicked switches and a monitor screen came foggily to life.

There was something odd on it, a strangely shaped object moving through nearby space.

Milo Clancey stared at the centre-section of Beacon Alpha Four for a moment before realizing what he was looking at. He hurried back to the chair and kicked the ancient rocket motors into life.

Jamie and Zoe were thrown about the cabin like a dice in a shaker while the Doctor held on with one hand and desperately struggled to shut down his magnetic lash-up with the other.

'Do something, Doctor,' yelled Zoe.

'I'm trying , I'm trying . . .'

The Doctor succeeded at last; the high-pitched howling died away and the cabin became still.

'Are we all right now?' gasped Jamie.

'I'm afraid not,' said the Doctor sadly. 'Even if I could manage to reverse the magnetic field we're too far from the other segments of the beacon to be attracted back.'

'So we're worse off than ever,' said Zoe sternly. 'Now we're just floating hopelessly in space.'

The Doctor looked contrite. 'I'm afraid we are. What a stupid blundering idiot I am!'

No one disagreed.

Warne's voice crackled from the communication unit in Madeleine Issigri's office.

'LIZ 79 is linked up with a section of Beacon Alpha Four. Request further orders.'

Hermack said triumphantly. 'You see? Clancey knew the collection zone. He's simply been waiting for the beacon sections to reach him.

'It could be coincidence, general' said Madeleine Issigri. Perhaps he just happened to spot the drifting wreckage.'

'And what are the odds against?' Hermack shook his head. 'This is the proof I needed. If I can use your communications unit again?'

Madeleine Issigri nodded, and Hermack leaned forward over the microphone.

'V-Master to Minnow Twenty-one, are you receiving me?'

'Standing by for orders, general. LIZ 79 is just completing link-up.'

'Good,' said Hermack. 'That means he can't make any sudden move. Go in and arrest him, Ian.'

'Tell your man to be careful' warned Madeleine Issigri. 'Clancey's got a terrible temper – he could go up like glyceryl trinitrate.'

'V-Master to Minnow Twenty-one,' said Hermack. 'If Clancey shows any sign of resistance, you are authorized to use your missiles. Otherwise just escort him back here.'

Jamie and Zoe were slumped back, scarcely able to move. The Doctor divided the last squirt of oxygen between them.

'What about you?' whispered Zoe feebly.

'It's all right, my dear, I don't need as much as you do.' Which was true enough, reflected the Doctor. Nevertheless, lack of oxygen would kill him in the end, as it would Jamie and Zoe. It would just take a little longer.

Suddenly a loud, grinding thump came from outside.

'Somebody's locked on to us,' said the Doctor.

Bolts began dropping from the sealed door one by one.

Zoe was astonished. 'Somebody's cutting the bolts from the outside!'

Jamie staggered to his feet. 'We've been found!'

A section of door fell away, and a bulky space-suited figure appeared covering them with a blaster rifle.

Jamie knew a weapon when he saw one and he reacted instantly.

'Oh no you don't!' he yelled, and sprang to the attack.

'Jamie, stop!' yelled the Doctor, but it was too late.

There was a fierce crackle of energy from the blaster and Jamie fell . . .

'Murderer!' shrieked Zoe.

The blaster rifle swung round to cover her . . .

7

Missile Attack

General Hermack was talking to the flight deck of his V-ship from Madeleine Issigri's office. '. . . and there's a possibility Major Warne may need assistance. I want you to stand-off at about twenty miles in case Clancey tries any tricks during the landing.'

The duty officer's voice came back. 'Very good, sir.'

If Madeleine Issigri resented having her office taken over as an unofficial Space Corps headquarters she gave no sign of it.

'Aren't you going back to your ship, general?'

'No, I'm looking after ground reception. I've kept back a section of guards equipped with short-range missiles.'

'All this for one old man? You're not taking any chances are you?'

'That's why I'm a general, ma'am.'

'What will happen to Milo?'

'He'll be taken back to Earth for trial.'

'You know, I can't help feeling sorry for him,' Madeleine Issigri said thoughtfully. 'I tried to buy him out years ago. I offered him enough to retire to Earth in luxury, but he refused. He's a stubborn old fool.'

Major Warne abruptly came through on the communicator. 'Minnow Twenty-one to V-Master. Clancey's ship is berthed against the beacon section.'

'Challenge him, and order him to surrender!'

There was a brief, tense pause before Warne's voice came again. 'No audio response from LIZ 79, sir.'

'Challenge him again. Fire warning rockets if you get no response within two minutes. If that doesn't work, stand off and destroy him with the Martian missiles.'

Warne glanced at the scanner screen in the cockpit of his minnow-ship. The screen was filled with a close-up of LIZ 79 berthed against the beacon segment.

'This is Space Fleet minnow fighter to LIZ 79. You have two minutes to surrender. Do you read me, Clancey? You have two minutes to surrender before I blow you into space.'

Inside LIZ 79 the message blared from a wall speaker. The cabin, however, was empty.

The Doctor was kneeling by the unconscious Jamie. 'It's all right, Zoe, he's coming round.'

'Of course he's coming round,' growled Milo

Clancey. 'The blaster's only set on stun. Now, I want to know who you are and what you are doing here.'

He waved the blaster rifle threateningly.

'It's very rude to point,' said Zoe severely. 'Especially with a gun.'

'How did you all get here?' demanded Milo exasperatedly. 'Where's your ship? You must have docked on to the beacon . . .'

'Not so much on as in,' said the Doctor cautiously.

'In it? Now how could you be doing that, it's impossible!'

Painfully, Jamie sat up. 'Nothing's impossible in the TARDIS, especially when the Doctor's at the controls.'

'You really expect me to believe this nonsense?' demanded Clancey. 'Now look, if you three comedians don't start telling me the truth . . .'

The whole beacon segment was rocked by a shattering explosion from the first of the minnow-ship's warning shots.

'Tarnation, someone's shooting at us!' said Milo Clancey indignantly.

He turned and dashed through the gap he had blown in the wall.

'Hey, wait for us!' shouted the Doctor.

He bustled Jamie and Zoe out after Clancey.

Too agitated to question their presence, Milo Clancey let them follow him on board. He closed the airlock behind them, and then led the way into the flight cabin, where Warne's voice was crackling from an antiquated speaker.

'That was just a warning, Clancey. You can't

hope to get away. Surrender or I'll put a missile salve through your hull.'

Ripping off his helmet, Milo hurled himself into the pilot's seat. 'It's that puppy from the Space Corps, is it? I'll show him a thing or two.'

He heaved and thumped at the controls, and the ancient rocket motors roared into life.

'I can see you moving, Clancey,' said Warne's voice from the speaker. 'I'll give you ten seconds to surrender. Ten seconds and then I fire!'

'Ten seconds, is it?' muttered Clancey. 'The nerve of the lad, talking to *me* like that!'

The voice started counting. 'Ten . . . nine . . . eight . . .'

'Don't you think it might be wise to, er, parley with him?' suggested the Doctor nervously.

'Milo Clancey takes ultimatums from no man!'

'Seven . . . six . . . five . . .'

Zoe looked at Clancey in horror. 'He's going to fire a missile!'

'I've a trick for that young whippersnapper worth ten missiles,' boasted Clancey. He heaved on a rusty lever.

Major Warne's minnow-ship was in close pursuit of the fleeing LIZ 79. The ancient vessel was clear on his scanner screen and in his missile sights.

'Four . . . three . . . two . . . one!' concluded Warne. 'Sorry, Clancey, you had your chance.' His thumb stabbed the firing button; the slender-finned missile streaked away from his ship straight at LIZ 79. It was point blank range; there was no possibility of a miss.

Suddenly the astonished Warne saw a dense

cloud of needle-like particles streaming from under the tail of the fleeing vessel. He watched in amazement as the missile entered the cloud and began pitching and rolling uncontrollably, deviating from its course and streaking uselessly into space.

He was even more amazed when his minnow-ship entered the cloud and began behaving in exactly the same way.

He wrestled furiously with the controls.

Milo Clancey brought the rear scanner into focus and chuckled gleefuly at the sight of the wildly-spinning minnow-ship. 'So much for you and your newfangled toy. Get yourself out of that Sunny Jim!'

His recently acquired passengers were looking at him with new respect.

'What did you do to him, Mr Clancey?' asked Zoe.

'Sure, that was me own invention, girl. A few tons of copper needles – I just tip them out when one of these modern ships gets too close for me peace of mind!'

Jamie was equally impressed. 'Och, how can copper needles stop a spaceship and a missile?'

Milo sprawled back in his chair. 'Well, they've both got these computerized guidance systems, haven't they? The argonite in their casings attracts the copper, then all the little copper needles jigger up the computer systems!'

'What's argonite?' asked Zoe.

'It's a metal used in spaceships,' said the Doctor. 'It's tensile, ductile, heatproof, almost indestructible – and magnetically polarized for copper!'

'That's right!' Milo looked at Zoe. 'And you've never heard of it, girl? Where do you come from?'

'Well, it's a little complicated,' began the Doctor. He told Milo about the TARDIS, and about the way they had lost contact with it.

Milo shook his head in wonder. 'Well, if that doesn't beat performing fleas!'

'So you can understand, Mr Clancey,' concluded the Doctor, 'we're very anxious to get back to the TARDIS. Would it be taking you too far out of your way to, um, drop us off?'

'Sure, I couldn't even if I wanted to. I don't know where the bits of the beacon are headed. Only the argonite pirates will know that.'

'Pirates?' asked Jamie. Milo told them about the recent run of argonite hijackings.

'Dear me,' said the Doctor. 'That does make things a little difficult.'

Milo turned his mind back to the present problems. 'We've got to get away from here. General Hermack will be sending more of his minnow-ships after us, and I've used up all me needles!' He told them about his recent brush with the Space Corps. 'Hermack's here hunting the space pirates – and he thinks I'm one of them.'

'There's one thing I still don't understand, Mr Clancey,' said Zoe.

'Sure, there's a million things I don't understand, girl, but I don't stand around asking daft questions about them!' He looked hopefully at her. 'You can make some tea if you like!'

Zoe took a deep breath. 'The pot's broken!' said Jamie hurriedly. He picked up the fragments of china on the deck.

58

Milo was already busy at the controls. 'There's another in the galley. That'll be okay – it's made of tillium.'

'What's tillium?' asked Zoe.

Milo slammed a fist down on the control console. 'Tillium! The metal this space-ship's made of. Makes a lousy cup of tea, but it's lasted me all round the galaxy.'

'So that's why your own ship wasn't affected by the copper needles! *That's* what I couldn't understand.' Her scientific curiosity satisfied, Zoe went off to look for the teapot.

'What will happen if those minnow-ships catch us?' asked Jamie.

'They won't laddie. I'm heading for the one place that bone-headed general will never think of looking.'

'He used some kind of anti-pursuit device, sir,' said Warne apologetically. 'It jammed the missile's guidance systems and the ship's as well.'

'Are you still tracking his ship.'

'No, sir. Sonar and radar are out of action. I can't do anything but sit here. Request immediate assistance, sir.'

'Request noted,' said Hermack coldly. The crestfallen figure on the screen disappeared.

Madeleine Issigri was handing a stack of cassettes to her secretary. 'Projected production figures and loading dates – get them out right away.' She turned to General Hermack as the secretary left. 'I gather Milo Clancey has escaped, general?'

Hermack nodded. 'May I monopolize your communication channel for a little longer?' he said stiffly.

'Yes, of course, general.'

A few moments later Penn's face was on the screen. 'Yes, general?'

'Were you monitoring Major Warne's last message?'

'Some of it, sir. There was a lot of interference.'

'I want the rest of the minnow-ships launched immediately. Milo Clancey's ship is to be found and destroyed!'

8

The Fugitives

Milo Clancey's old ship was roaring through space like a runaway express train, vibrating so fiercely that it seemed in danger of shaking itself to pieces.

'I feel a wee bit sick, Doctor,' whispered Jamie.

'Willpower, Jamie, willpower,' said the Doctor, who seemed quite unaffected by the motion.

'More tea anyone?' asked Zoe brightly.

Milo looked up from the controls. 'I'll have some if there's any left.'

Zoe poured him some in his battered mug, and the Doctor passed it to him. 'I've been watching your pressure gauge, Mr Clancey. Rather high, isn't it?'

'Aye, just a bit. Thermopile's wearing out, nothing I can do.'

'Except slow down?' suggested the Doctor. 'I mean, there could be a very nasty explosion!'

'Don't worry, Doctor, LIZ is a tough old girl. They don't build ships like this today, you know!'

'I'm glad to hear it,' muttered Jamie.

'Never you mind, laddie, not far to go now.'

'Where are we going?' asked Zoe.

Milo punched a control and a mist-shrouded planet emerged on the scanner screen. 'That's where we're going: Ta!'

The Doctor peered at the screen. 'Is it inhabited?'

'It is now. It's the headquarters of the Issigri Mining Corporation.'

'And why won't the Space Corps look for you there?' asked Jamie sceptically.

Milo chuckled. 'Because Madeleine Issigri, the president of the corporation, is my sworn enemy. It's the one place Hermack expects me to stay away from!'

The Doctor looked puzzled. 'If this lady is your enemy, won't she hand you over to the Space Corps?'

'She won't know we're here, Doctor. I shan't be announcing me arrival.'

Zoe studied the image of the planet on the scanner. It was much closer now, and she could make out more surface detail. 'It seems to be just a desert.'

'Sure, there's not much surface life on Ta – too much ultra-violet. Everything's underground, and that's where we'll be, if I can find my old landing pad.'

'I gather you've been here before?' said the Doctor.

'Me and me old partner Dom Issigri, rest his

soul, turned this planet into Swiss cheese between us. Richest argonite field we ever struck, took us ten years to clean it out.' Milo bent over the scanner, which showed the dusty, cratered surface of the planet. 'Now where's that entry shaft . . .'

General Hermack bowed stiffly. 'Goodbye, Madame Issigri, and many thanks for your hospitality.'

'Where are you heading now, General?'

'First I have to pull Major Warne out of the fix he's got himself into. Then I have to pick up the men I've stationed on the beacons. And after that – Lobos!'

'Milo Clancey's base?'

'The argonite pirate's base,' corrected Hermack. 'It's my guess that the beacon segments are heading there. With any luck we can catch Clancey redhanded and clean out the whole operation.'

'I hope so, general. My freighter crews are demanding to be armed in case they're attacked.'

Hermack's eye was caught by a beautifully made model of a spaceship mounted on a stand. 'A Beta Dart!'

'The company's just bought two, general. We use them for express freight.'

'It's as well you told me. The pirates are using a Beta Dart as well. I'd hate to knock out one of yours by mistake.'

Madeleine Issigri smiled, tapping the striped nose-cone of the Dart. 'All our freighters have the Issigri nose-cone – I designed it myself.'

'Very distinctive,' said Hermack drily. 'What does a Beta Dart cost?'

'Upwards of a hundred million credits. Why?'

'I was wondering where Clancey got his hands on that kind of money. Still, he could easily have made that much and more from selling his stolen argonite. There's an illicit market on Roja Four . . .'

Madeleine Issigri said worriedly: 'Are you sure you're right about Milo Clancey, general?'

'Positive! And believe me, if those beacon sections are on course for Lobos when I find them, Milo Clancey won't live long enough to enjoy his money!'

LIZ 79 thumped to the bottom of the underground landing shaft with all the grace of a lead balloon.

Milo Clancey looked round. 'Nice smooth landing, that time!'

The Doctor and his companions picked themselves up.

'Smooth?' said Jamie, rubbing the back of his kilt. 'I'd like to know what you'd call rough!'

Milo laughed. 'Soft, are you, boy?'

Jamie glared furiously at him, 'Just let me get my feet on solid ground and we'll see who's soft!'

'There'll be no solid ground for you, laddie, nor your friends. You're all going to stay here in the ship where you're safe.'

'Why do you want us to stay here?' asked the Doctor mildly.

'We're in an abandoned freighter dock a mile underground. There's nothing out there to see and nowhere to go, just a maze of argonite tunnels. Get lost in them and even I might not find you.'

Grabbing a toolbag, Milo headed for the door.

'In that case, may I ask where *you're* going, Mr Clancey?'

'To check the damage from that warning rocket,' said Clancey. He disappeared through the doorway.

Jamie watched him go. 'Do you think we can trust him, Doctor?'

'I think we have to, Jamie. We've no chance of finding the TARDIS if we leave this ship.'

'Do we have a chance anyway? It's on one of those bits of beacon and we don't know where they're heading.'

'The space pirates must have a blast furnace to melt down the argonite,' said the Doctor thoughtfully.' Unfortunately, there's no way we can even guess where their headquarters might be.'

Zoe had been sitting quietly in a corner, working on a sheet of calculations. 'We don't have to guess, Doctor. It's simple enough to work out.'

She showed him her calculations. 'This is the position of our beacon section when Milo first saw it, and this is our position eight minutes when he boarded. I got the figures from Milo's computer. With that data it's not difficult to work out the original position and course of the beacon's fragments.'

The Doctor frowned at the calculations. 'Ah but what about my little experiment with electro-magnetism?'

'Oh, I compensated for that. Look! electromagnetic waves are always at right-angles to the direction of propagation, and as you know they travel at 186,282 miles a second.'

'I see. Well, Zoe, what's the answer?'

'If we'd stayed on our original course, we would eventually have landed somewhere very close to where we are now!'

'Bless my soul!' said the Doctor. 'You're quite right. It's a simple enough calculation as you say, Zoe. I wonder why I didn't think of it myself!'

'So do I, Doctor,' said Zoe innocently.

Jamie had been struggling to follow what was going on. 'Doctor, are you saying that the TARDIS is going to land near where we are now?'

'Yes, Jamie, isn't it splendid?'

'Aye, but that means the pirates must be right here as well.'

'So Milo must be one of them after all,' said Zoe. 'That's why he landed here!'

The Doctor came to a decision.' If the TARDIS is going to be landing near here, we've got to find it. Come on – and don't make a noise going down the ladder.'

'Right!' said Jamie. He dashed for the door, tripped over a chair and came down with a crash.

The Doctor and Zoe looked reproachfully at him.

'Aye, well,' said Jamie defensively. 'We're no on the ladder yet!'

They crept out of the cabin.

In an underground chamber filled with communications equipment the lean, dark man called Caven sat watching a bank of monitor screens.

He swung round in his chair as his number two hurried into the room. 'Ah, Dervish, there you are.'

'All right, Caven, what's the panic?'

'No panic, Dervish,' said Caven softly. 'I wanted to talk to you. How are things going at the plant?'

66

'I'm just starting on the last section of Alpha Two.'

'Leave it. Suledin can take charge. I want you to take the ship out. The Alpha Four sections are to be rerouted to Lobos.

'That's impossible!'

Caven's voice was softer than ever. 'When I give an order, Dervish, don't ever say it's impossible.'

'Do you realize how far it is to Lobos? We'd have to refuel the beacon rockets.'

'That's exactly what I want you to do.'

'Caven, listen,' pleaded Dervish. 'The Space Corps is out there looking for us, with a V-ship and a flight of minnow-ships. It's too dangerous! I won't do it . . .'

Caven drew the holstered blaster that never left his side. 'Keep arguing with me, Dervish, and Suledin will be taking over your job permanently.'

'I was only pointing out the dangers, Caven.'

Caven's voice dropped to a whisper. 'You're in more danger here and now than you'll ever find in space . . .'

Suddenly a light flashed and a voice came from the console. 'Intruders in perimeter tunnel nine.'

Caven flicked a switch. 'Alert all guards. I'm, on my way.'

'The Space Corps!' gasped Dervish.

'I don't know. Whoever it is, we'll deal with them in the tunnels. Now get moving!'

The Doctor, Jamie and Zoe were making their way along a dark, dank tunnel. The walls were rough-hewn, with many cracks and fissures. From somewhere in the distance came the sound of dripping water.

'I don't think this can be the right way,' whispered Zoe. 'We seem to be going deeper.'

'What do you think, Doctor?' said Jamie. 'Should we turn back?'

'I'm beginning to think we should have listened to Mr Clancey, Jamie. He said we'd get lost, and we . . .' The Doctor broke off. 'I thought I heard something – a sort of buzzing noise.'

'I can hear it too, but I canna tell where it's coming from.'

The Doctor cocked his head. 'It seems to be somewhere above us.'

'There's a wee light up there, too. It seems to be coming from that crack in the roof.'

'The light must be coming through from the other side,' said the Doctor. 'Unfortunately, it's far too high to reach.'

'I'm the lightest,' said Zoe. 'Lift me up – maybe I can see through.'

'Good idea,' said the Doctor. 'Make a back, Jamie.'

'Aye, it's always me,' grumbled Jamie. He bent down, and the Doctor helped Zoe climb first on to Jamie's back, and then on to his shoulders.

Jamie slowly stood up. Zoe supported herself against the wall and put an eye to the fissure.

A moment later the Doctor helped her scramble down. 'Well, Zoe?'

'There are two men there working with machinery. I think you were right, Jamie, the pirates are here too!'

'Are you sure they weren't miners?'

Zoe shook her head.' They weren't mining, Doctor. They were cutting up metal into scrap – it looked very like part of a beacon!'

'Then we've stumbled on to the space pirates' hideout. That buzzing must be their electric furnaces.'

A beam of light suddenly struck them.

Screwing up his eyes, the Doctor saw that it was a portable searchlight carried by two men. There seemed to be other men behind them – men with guns.

The little group instinctively backed away.

A metallic voice shouted: 'Back you go. Keep moving!'

The Doctor stood his ground. 'Now really,' he protested, 'there's no need to . . .'

A blaster chipped a chunk of rock from the wall by his feet. The Doctor skipped back.

'Keep moving!' shouted the voice.

Another bit of rock splintered from the rock wall by Jamie's head.

'Hey!' yelled Jamie.

'Back! shouted the shadowy figure behind the searchlight. 'Back! Back! Back!'

Zoe turned and saw a small round hole in the wall behind her.

'Quick, Doctor, through here!'

She leaped through the opening – and gave a yell of alarm.

Jamie ran after her and then teetered on the edge of the opening. Beyond it was a sheer drop into darkness.

'Keep back, Doctor,' yelled Jamie. 'It's some kind of pit!'

But the Doctor was already on Jamie's heels. He grabbed Jamie's hand just as the young Highlander lost his balance and fell. The Doctor was dragged after him.

Struggling furiously, they dropped down into blackness.

9

The Prisoners

The Doctor, Jamie and Zoe landed one by one at
the bottom of the shaft.

Zoe instinctively rolled over as she hit the
ground. Jamie narrowly missed her, falling heavily
close to one side.

The Doctor, however, landed partly on top of
Jamie provoking a yell of protest.

Gradually they sorted themselves out.

'Doctor, are you all right?' gasped Zoe.

'No,' said the Doctor sadly. He fished in the
back pocket of his baggy chequered trousers and
produced a broken cardboard box of drawing pins.
'I like drawing pins – usually.'

Jamie tried to get up, and winced with pain. 'I
think I've twisted my ankle.'

The Doctor helped him up. 'Can you stand,
Jamie?'

Jamie limped a few paces backward and forward.

'Aye, it's no so bad.' He looked round. 'Now then where are we?'

They were in semi-darkness: the pit seemed to be lit by only the faint light from the tunnel above.

They looked round, trying to accustom their eyes to the gloom.

'It looks a bit like a prison cell,' said Zoe.

The Doctor nodded. 'I think this is where they were driving us anyway . . .'

A low moan came from somewhere in the dark recesses of the pit. Raising a hand for silence, the Doctor moved cautiously forward, Jamie close behind him.

The Doctor saw a shadowy figure stretched out in the corner, and knelt beside it.

As he came closer, Jamie saw that the figure was in uniform. 'I think it's one of those men from the beacon, Doctor, the ones that were firing at us.'

The Doctor finished his examination. 'His shoulder's been hit by an energy-bolt, but I don't think it's broken.' Looking round, the Doctor saw an earthenware jug half full of water. He dipped his handkerchief in it and used the damp cloth to moisten the unconscious man's lips and forehead.

The man moaned and stirred, his eyelids fluttering open.

From his hidden control room, Caven was talking to Dervish, now reluctantly in space on the pirates' Beta Dart.

The face on the vid-com screen was sweating with fear.

'I'm returning to base, Caven, you hear me? I'm bringing the ship back.'

'Calm down, man,' said Caven gently. 'What's your position?'

'We're forty-three thousand miles out, on an intersection course with the beacon segments.'

'You'll be among them in minutes then. What's the panic?'

'We're running into a trap. Our scanners have picked up the Space Corps cruiser just over two hours away on a convergent course!'

Caven considered. 'How long will it take you to get those beacon sections diverted to Lobos?'

'At least two hours, maybe more. We just can't do it before the cruiser gets in range.'

'You'll have to work quickly then, won't you Dervish. Find some way to cut the time.'

'We can't, I tell you. The battle-cruiser will send minnows to blast us to bits. I'm coming back.'

Caven held up a simple hand control, plugged into the panel. 'I'm sure you recognize this, Dervish? After all you helped to design it.'

'It's a UHF detonator.'

'That's right, and it's keyed to a charge under your atomic drive.'

'I don't believe you. You're bluffing.'

'If you think I'm bluffing, Dervish, just try turning back. You've got a fair chance of escaping the Space Corps, but you've no chance at all of getting away from me.'

The Doctor and his companions were exchanging stories with their fellow captive, who turned out to be a Space Corps lieutenant called Sorba. He had been captured by Caven and his men during the attack on Beacon Alpha Four.

The Doctor was already planning his escape. 'There's obviously a less painful way of getting in here – which means there must also be a way out.'

'There's no way out, believe me,' said Sorba wearily. 'I've searched every inch.'

Zoe looked curiously at the Doctor. 'Why are you so certain, Doctor. This place could just be a sort of tomb, a burial pit.'

The Doctor tapped the earthenware jug. 'Water, in a fairly fragile jug. It couldn't just have been dropped down that shaft, now could it?'

He started tapping the walls.

Working under the threat of death, Dervish's men had shown an amazing turn of speed – and made an astonishing discovery.

Dervish reported back to Caven on the vid-com link. 'I've got crews refuelling the rockets and realigning them for Lobos, but there are only seven sections here now. The main one, the eighth, has completely disappeared. There's no sign of debris either. Someone must have engineered it out of its flight-path.'

Caven thought hard. 'That Space Corps man we took off the beacon was babbling about other people on board. Maybe someone's trying to cut themselves in. I'll question him, find out what he saw. You get on with the job, Dervish, and report as soon as those sections are on their new course.'

Sorba watched disbelievingly as Jamie and the Doctor went round the pit, solemnly tapping every inch of wall. 'They're mad, it's solid rock I tell you!'

Zoe smiled. 'When the Doctor gets an idea it's very hard to change his mind.'

By now Jamie was beginning to get discouraged. 'Och, this is hopeless, Doctor.'

'Patience, Jamie, patience!' The Doctor produced a stethoscope and started listening to the wall. 'Now, wait a second . . . Yes, I think there's a control unit just about . . . here!' He produced a piece of chalk and drew a little circle on the wall.

Jamie gave him a worried look. 'What do you think's under there?'

'It's probably an audio-lock. They became very popular after burglars started carrying mini-computers.' The Doctor was searching through his many pockets. 'The question is, what have I done with my tuning fork . . . Ah, success!'

Delightedly, the Doctor held up an old-fashioned tuning fork, and began tapping it gently against the wall inside the chalked circle.

Jamie turned worriedly to Zoe and whispered: 'Do you think he landed on his head when he fell down the shaft?'

Penn looked up from his scanner screen. 'Contact, sir. Seven objects moving quite slowly.'

Warne frowned. 'If it's the beacon, there should be eight.'

'What's their course?' demanded Hermack.

'The same as ours, sir.'

'Lobos!' said Hermack exultantly. 'Clancey's home base. We've got him!'

'There's something moving on the edge of frame, sir,' reported Penn suddenly.

'Is it the missing section?'

'No, sir, it's too big and it's moving too fast. It must be a ship.'

'It's the pirates,' said Hermack. 'A ship out here, it's got to be! Major Warne, get down to the minnow deck. I want you ready to go as soon as we get identification of that ship.'

As Warne hurried away, Hermack turned to Penn. 'You can forget those beacon sections – our target is that ship!'

A few minutes later Warne came through from the minnow deck. 'I'm in Minnow Twenty-two ready to go, general. Any news?'

'Penn has just made a positive identification. The ship's definitely a Beta Dart. It can still outrun us.'

'It won't outrun a minnow,' said Warne grimly.

'She's boosting, sir,' called Penn. 'She must have spotted us!'

Hermack leaned forward eagerly. 'V-Master to Minnow Twenty-two. Blast away, Ian!'

'Right, sir. I'll bring you back a chunk for a souvenir!'

Seconds later, the sleek, deadly minnow blasted away from the mother ship into the blackness of deep space.

Caven summoned a guard into the control room. 'There's a Space Corps lieutenant in the cell under tunnel nine. I want him brought here for questioning. Here's the key to the audio-lock.'

The guard hurried away just as Dervish's worried face came up on the vid-com screen.

'We've got a minnow-ship on our tail. We're on maximum boost, but it's closing fast.'

'Try to shake it off long enough to reach the nose cone.'

Warne's voice came through to the flight deck. 'I've just lost contact. Can you steer me?'

Penn looked at the scanner screen, where the two blips were slowly moving apart.

He looked up at General Hermack. 'Major Warne's lost her, sir, she's doubling round. Minnow Twenty-two, do you read me?'

'Loud and clear!'

'Steer thirty-seven degrees port . . .'

As Penn reeled off a string of co-ordinates, steering the minnow by remote control, the blips started to converge.

A striped nose-cone hung in space ahead of the frantically-twisting Beta Dart.

The Beta Dart manoeuvred straight on to it, so that the nose-cone locked on to the front of the ship.

'Beta Dart now on visual scanners,' reported Warne.

'Switch video through,' ordered Hermack.

Relayed from the minnow, the image of the Beta Dart came up on the battle-cruiser's screen.

Hermack stared unbelievingly at the striped nose-cone. 'That's an Issigri ship! Minnow Twenty-two, flash out! I repeat, flash out!'

A moment of tense silence, then Warne's voice came through, 'Contact lost, sir.'

'You didn't fire at her?' demanded Hermack.

'No, sir. I had her in my sights when I got your order. What went wrong?'

'You nearly wiped out an Issigri mining freighter, Ian!'

Warne sounded baffled and resentful. 'If it wasn't a pirate ship, sir, why did they run? And why are they still running? They've just disappeared at maximum boost . . .'

Hermack wearily shook his head. 'I don't know. We'll have to abort the mission, Ian. You'd better come in.'

Turning away from the screen, Hermack stared thoughtfully into space.

10

Escape

The steady ping! ping! ping! of the Doctor's tuning fork was beginning to drive his fellow prisoners crazy.

'Doctor, will you no give it a rest,' pleaded Jamie.

The Doctor was indignant. 'You want to get out of here, don't you?'

'Och, that'll never get us out!'

'It will if I can hit the right key,' said the Doctor obstinately. 'An audio-lock can be activated only by a particular sound. So far I haven't managed to find it.'

He gave a further succession of twangs.

'I canna bear it any more!' shouted Jamie suddenly. Snatching the tuning fork from the Doctor's hand he hurled it at the rock wall. The tuning fork gave out a particularly jarring twang, there was a heavy grating sound, and a section of wall slid back before their astonished eyes.

'Well done, Jamie,' said the Doctor delightedly, 'You've found the right key!'

Jamie and Zoe turned to help the astonished Lieutenant Sorba to his feet.

'Come on,' said Zoe. 'We can get away now!'

'I'm not so sure,' said the Doctor worriedly.

Zoe and Jamie turned to see that there was an armed man on the other side of the door.

The man stepped forward. To their utter astonishment it was Milo Clancey.

'I've been trying to find the way into this cell for half an hour. Come along with you now!'

Nobody moved, and Milo glared indignantly at them. 'What's the matter with you? You're not still thinking I'm in cahoots with the pirates?'

'It might help if you pointed that weapon in another direction,' said the Doctor.

Milo slung the blaster rifle over his shoulder. 'Now listen to me, all of you! The only reason you're locked up here now is because you did just what I told you not to do and ran away into the tunnels. I've had the devil of a job finding you, and if you do want to get out of here alive, Milo Clancey's the only fellow can show you the way! So, are you coming, or am I leaving you to rot?'

'Ah well, if you put it like that . . .' said the Doctor.

'Good, it's about time you showed a mite of sense. 'Milo looked at Sorba. 'Who's this?'

'His name's Sorba,' explained Jamie. 'The pirates took him prisoner when they attacked the beacon.'

'I've not much time for the Space Corps! Still, I suppose we'll have to take him with us.'

'Listen!' said the Doctor. 'Someone's coming . . .'

They heard heavy footsteps coming towards them.

'The door's open!' shouted an astonished voice, and an armed guard appeared out of the darkness.

Milo swung the rifle from his shoulder and shot him down. He fired at the second guard and missed; the man turned and fled down the corridor with Milo after him.

Sorba nodded towards the prone guard. 'Grab his gun, boy, it might be useful.'

As Jamie picked up the gun Milo puffed wearily back to the cell door. 'A few years ago I'd have caught him before he got ten yards.'

'He got away from you?'

'He did, he did, Doctor. Now there'll be guards buzzing round these corridors like a swarm of bees.'

'Then we'd better leave,' said Zoe practically.

'We had indeed,' said Milo. 'I'll lead the way.'

They heard the distant wailing of a siren.

'The alarm,' said Milo. 'What did I tell you? Come on!'

Caven was directing the hunt from his control room.

'They're through into the workings on level eight,' a voice reported.

'I told you to seal off the lower caverns.'

'We did, but somehow they got past us. They seem to know their way round better than we do.'

'I want these people caught or killed,' snarled Caven. 'And I don't much care which, understand?'

81

Another voice called: 'They've just passed the perimeter video eye on level six!'

'Level six already,' muttered Caven. He raised his voice. 'I want every available man up to level three. Use the elevators. I want every entrance to that level sealed off. I'm coming down – and it had better be done by the time I get there.'

As he hurried from the control room, one name was running through Caven's mind. 'Milo Clancey!' he muttered. 'There's only one man who could find his way through these tunnels like that. It's got to be Milo Clancey.'

Milo was setting a cracking pace through the tunnels, up cramped iron ladders and along disused ventilator shafts. His followers were soon exhausted.

Sorba, still weak from his wound, had to be almost carried.

'We'll have to stop for a bit,' said Jamie.

'I'm all right,' muttered Sorba weakly.

'Aye, mebbe. But I'm not!'

'I need a rest anyway,' said Zoe firmly. 'All this running and climbing . . .'

'Well, just for a minute,' said Milo reluctantly. 'But remember all the time we're stopped, they'll be closing in!'

He led them down to a side tunnel, where an old electrical junction box hung drunkenly from the wall. Its door was dangling from one hinge, revealing a jumble of rusty electronic circuits.

Boxes of abandoned equipment provided seats, and they settled down to rest.

'Where are we making for, Mr Clancey?' asked the Doctor.

'The Issigri Mining Corporation. It's only another two levels to its headquarters.'

'But didn't you say its president was your sworn enemy?'

Milo sighed. 'Madeleine Issigri, aye. Dom Issigri, her father, was my old partner. He disappeared here years ago and she blames me for his death. Me – and I wasn't even here!'

'Then what makes you think she'll help you now?'

'When I found you'd all skedaddled from the LIZ, I guessed what had happened and followed you down into these tunnels. I was there when you got captured. And I saw the leader of these space pirates – Maurice Caven! That's when it all fell into place.'

The Doctor frowned. 'You know this man?'

'I know him for a thieving murderous criminal. We clashed in the old days: he was a notorious claim-jumper. I had him put away in the end, handed him over to the Space Corps myself. He broke out of the penal colony, and went on to bigger and worse things.'

'How do you mean it all fell into place?'

'Well, I've always felt this piracy business was aimed at *me*! My freighters got hit the most, and on top of that there were these rumours I was behind it all. It was as though someone wanted to put me out of business.' Milo laughed. 'Sure, for a while I even suspected little Maddy herself.'

'But now you think that someone is this man Caven?'

'I'm sure it is. He always hated me, always swore he'd have his revenge. When I tell Madeleine he's down here in her mines . . .'

Jamie interrupted them. 'Hey, I can hear someone coming.'

They all jumped up, all except Sorba who had been lying stretched out by the wall. He tried to struggle to his feet, but slumped back. 'It's no use, I'll never make it. You go on.'

Milo glared down at him. 'I've brought you this far, laddie; I'm not leaving you now.'

'We can carry him between us, Milo,' said the Doctor quietly. 'But it's going to slow us down.'

Zoe was listening to the sounds from down the tunnel. 'They're not far behind us now.'

Jamie's face was full of the joy of battle. 'Aye? Well don't worry, they'll no get much further.'

Clutching the blaster rifle he'd taken from the guard, he ran back down the tunnel.

'He won't keep them back for ever,' said Milo practically. 'He's got no recharge units for that gun.'

The Doctor was studying the box hanging from the wall. 'I take it this is some kind of power distributor box, Mr Clancey?'

Milo nodded. 'There's one for every level.'

'The question is, are they still connected . . .' The Doctor jiggled some wires, producing a bang and a flash and a shower of blue sparks.

'It's still connected, Doctor,' said Zoe. 'Now what?'

'That depends what we can lay our hands on!' The Doctor began rummaging through the boxes of equipment.

Jamie had a natural talent with any kind of weapon and the blaster rifle was easy enough to use: set the power-level, press a firing-stud, and the thing projected an energy bolt.

Setting the power to maximum, Jamie took cover behind a convenient pile of rocks and waited for his foes to come within range.

The first shadowy figure appeared down the tunnel. Jamie fired, and the man dropped with a yell. The others fell back.

Jamie fired again. This time his fire was returned and a chunk of rock exploded by his head.

He ducked back into cover, then popped up and fired again.

The Doctor had found a coil of metal cable and was frantically connecting one end to the junction box while Zoe unwound the rest of the wire across the tunnel.

'Fasten the wire to the metal ring in the far wall there, Zoe. Then trail the wire across the floor and lead it back again.'

Milo looked on in amazement. 'What's that contraption supposed to do – trip them up?'

A guard tried to wriggle forwards; Jamie stopped him dead with a blaster-bolt.

Another tried a charge, and Jamie dropped him on the run.

The leader of the space pirates rose to wave his men on.

Jamie took careful aim – and found to his disgust that the gun was dead.

Tossing it aside, he ran back down the tunnel.

'Everyone back behind those wires,' said the Doctor, and threw the switch.

There was a faint hum of power, but that was all.

'Well, I *think* it's working,' said the Doctor dubiously.

Jamie came hurtling down the tunnel towards him. 'Run, everyone, run! They're coming!'

'Wait, Jamie!' yelled the Doctor and leaped for the switch, throwing it seconds before Jamie hit the cat's-cradle of wire laced across the tunnel floor.

Heaving Jamie past the wire, the Doctor threw the switch again and retreated down the tunnel.

Realizing that Jamie's weapon was exhausted, Caven's guards dashed confidently down the tunnel.

The guard in the lead suddenly twisted and fell in mid-air, sparks playing about his body.

Terrified by this new, unknown danger, the guards fell back.

Madeleine Issigri rose from behind her ornate desk in amazement as Milo Clancey and his motley companions were shown into her office by one of her guards.

'Milo, it really is you! I couldn't believe it when they told me you were here! And who are all these others? What's going on – and why have you stayed away so long?'

Milo Clancey strode masterfully forwards. He had known Madeleine Issigri since the day she was born. He still couldn't quite accept that she'd

86

grown up, let alone that she was now president of a rival mining company.

'Madeleine, my dear, will you do one thing for me before you start asking questions? I want you to contact General Hermack right away, and tell him to get that V-ship of his here just as soon as he can.'

'But he's only just left? Why should I call him back? What's so urgent?'

'There you go, asking questions again! Because you've a nest of vipers in your mine workings, that's why!'

Madeleine still looked baffled; the Doctor intervened.

'Mr Clancey means that argonite pirates have been using your tunnels as their secret hideout.'

'Argonite pirates? Here on on Ta – in my mines? Oh, really Milo!'

'You remember hearing of Maurice Caven, your father's old enemy and mine. You know what sort of villain he is? Well, it's him that's behind it, after revenge on me and as you as well.'

Madeleine Issigri seemed to realize that he was serious. 'If he is using the old mine workings as you say then my company guards will take care of him.'

'But he's got an army of armed cut-throats down there!'

'There's still no need to call in the Space Corps. My men will deal with them.'

'The girl's as stubborn as her old man,' said Milo despairingly. 'Your guards wouldn't stand a chance against Caven's mob. I'm calling the Space Corps whether you like it or not!' He strode towards the vid-com console beside the desk.

'Stop!' called Madeleine. 'Don't touch that console, Milo.'

Caven suddenly burst in, flanked by two armed men.

Sorba was the first to react. He snatched the blaster-rifle from Madeleine's guard and swung it round to cover Caven, who promptly blasted Sorba down before he could fire.

Caven smiled coldly. 'Anyone else want to die like a hero?'

11

Betrayed

Caven stepped carelessly over Sorba's body. 'You just walked in with your eyes wide open then, Clancey? How very naive of you!'

Raising his hand-blaster he aimed it at Milo's head. "I've waited for this a long time . . .'

Madeleine Issigri stepped forward. 'Wait! I never agreed to anything like this. Not to murder!'

Caven smiled. 'If it worries you, step outside for a moment – it won't take long.'

'Just remember, Caven, I'm running this operation.'

'Are you? I do all the dirty work, though. Space piracy, grand larceny . . .

'And the first degree homicides,' growled Clancey.

'Right, Clancey, let's not forget the homicides.' Caven turned back to Madeleine. 'While you sit and look pretty and count the money. But you're still just as guilty as I am.'

'I have never agreed to murder . . .'

'Well, you're going to have to agree now. Unless we get rid of these snoopers, we'll both end up in a nirvan chamber.'

'I don't want them killed,' said Madeleine firmly. 'There must be some other solution.'

'I should hope there is!' said the Doctor indignantly.

There was a long moment while Caven considered.

Milo could feel Jamie tensing beside him, and realized that he was planning to jump the nearest guard.

He gripped Jamie's arm. 'Steady lad, remember poor Sorba.'

Caven took his head guard aside and muttered briefly into his ear. He turned to Madeleine. 'I've told him to lock them up under the freighter dock complex. Satisfied?'

'What made you change your mind?'

'That Space Corps V-ship is becoming a nuisance. I've thought of a way to get rid of it.

At this precise moment the V-ship was in orbit around the planet Lobos.

Major Warne was off on a reconnaissance flight, reporting via the vid-com link to General Hermack on the flight deck.

'The beacon sections are still in orbit round Lobos, general, but there's no sign of anyone collecting them. I landed and checked out Clancey's base. His mining crew say he took off weeks ago and they've had no word of him since.'

'Were they telling the truth?'

'I thought so, sir. I also made a pretty close reconnaissance of the planet before landing. I saw no sign of a landing installation that could take that Beta Dart the pirates are using.'

'Naturally they'd camouflage it . . .'

'I checked for radiation traces as well, general, no way to camouflage them. I found nothing. I'd say Lobos has never been used by an atomic-drive ship. I think we've been side-tracked, sir. The beacon segments were diverted to lead us away from the pirates' real base.'

'Then we'll just have to find them. All right, Ian, mission concluded, back you come.'

'On my way, sir.'

As Warne's face vanished from the screen, Hermack turned to Penn. 'Have you got the beacon segments' original course from where we first picked them up?

'It's plotted on the computer, sir.'

'Can you project a destination from that data?'

Penn punched co-ordinates into a keyboard, and studied a read-out screen. 'On their original course, sir, the segments would have gone into orbit around the planet Ta.'

Caven's guards marched their prisoners along a steel corridor lined with heavy metal pipes and steel cables.

The party halted outside a heavy steel door. A guard unlocked it and swung it open while the head guard motioned them inside with his blaster.

'Has anyone got a light?' asked the Doctor mildly. 'It looks very dark in there.'

'Hurry up there,' snarled the guard. 'Inside!'

They were shoved through the door, which slammed shut behind them.

For a moment they stood in confusion in pitch darkness. The Doctor fished an old-fashioned red-tipped match from his pocket and lit it on his thumbnail, holding the light high above his head.

To their surprise they found themselves not in the bare cell they'd been expecting but in an elaborately furnished old-fashioned study.

There was a desk, a sofa and armchairs, and the walls were lined with handsomely-bound books. A grandfather clock ticked loudly in the corner.

There was a massive table covered with a fringed velvet cloth that hung down to the ground.

Above the antique fireplace was a framed portrait of a distinguished looking grey-haired man.

'It's Dom Issigri himself,' said Milo, 'Madeleine's father. This is his private study. It's years since I was in here.'

The Doctor's match burned low and he blew it out. 'I don't suppose you remember where the light-switch is?'

Milo chuckled. 'There isn't one, Doctor. He was an old-fashioned romantic was Dom. He had all this stuff brought from Earth. There might be a lamp or some candles. Try the corner cupboard.'

'Are these candles, Doctor?'

'Yes indeed, Zoe, a whole box of them. Well done!'

Soon there were several lighted candles dotted

about and they were able to study their strange surroundings.

'I'm surprised Caven put us in here,' said Milo. 'I heard Madeleine had the place locked up after Dom disappeared. Never came here herself and never let anyone else come either.'

'I think someone's been here fairly recently,' said the Doctor calmly. 'That clock in the corner has an eight-day movement, and it's still ticking.'

'Och, nobody would come down here just to wind a clock,' said Jamie.

'No, they wouldn't, would they,' said the Doctor thoughtfully.

He suddenly became aware that Zoe was tugging at his sleeve. She was looking downwards.

He followed the direction of her gaze and saw a scrawny, bare foot sticking out from under the edge of the tablecloth.

Picking up one of the candles, the Doctor crept towards the table and lifted up the cloth.

Cowering under the table, like a wild beast in a cave, was a ragged, unkempt old man.

Strangely enough, the Doctor recognized him at once. It was the man in the portrait – Dom Issigri, Madeleine's supposedly-dead father.

'Dervish has landed in your Beta Dart, by the way,' said Caven. 'He'll be coming up to report any minute now. Apparently the nose-cone idea worked a treat – it threw the Space Corps right off the scent.'

Madeleine was sitting behind her desk; Caven perched on the edge, very much at ease.

'How long for?' she asked. 'Hermack will soon

be back when he realizes there's nothing on Lobos. Isn't it time we operated the emergency plan?'

'Flood the tunnels and lose all our equipment?' Caven shook his head.

'If we don't we risk the Space Corps finding our illegal smelting plant and the stolen argonite. They'll ship us back to Earth for trial – and execution!'

Caven rose and stretched. There was something cat-like about him, thought Madeleine . . .

'Hermack still thinks Milo's behind the piracy,' said Caven. 'As it happens, we've just found that old freighter of his, the LIZ, on an old landing pad.'

'Well?'

'I'm going to have it fitted with remote control steering, fill the holds with stolen argonite, and put Clancey and all his friends on board. The LIZ will take off, apparently trying to escape, just as Hermack's V-ship comes in range.'

'So Hermack will pick them up, and they'll promptly tell him everything.

Caven shook his head. 'Don't worry – he won't get a word out of them.'

Madeleine suddenly understood what he meant. 'You're talking about deliberate murder, and that's something I'll never agree to.'

'I've got twice as many men on this planet as you have,' said Caven softly. 'And mine are all armed. I warn you, don't interfere!'

He turned as Dervish came into the room. 'Ah, there you are! We were just discussing a space accident.'

Dervish looked baffled. 'Where? When?'

94

Caven smiled. 'I haven't quite decided that yet!'

'I don't get it,' said Dervish uneasily.

'We've got Clancey's old ship. I want you to fit her up with a remote control guidance system.'

Dervish shrugged. 'If you say so.'

'It's a very old ship,' said Caven softly. 'Did I say that? Practically falling apart. I want the oxygen pump rigged so it does full apart, say about five minutes after take-off?'

Dom Issigri crouched in a corner of the room, hands over his face, cowering away from the candle flame.

So far, all the Doctor's attempts to reassure him had met with no success. The old man just cringed back, wedging himself into his corner.

'You go and talk to him, Milo,' said the Doctor. 'Just talk to him quietly about anything you can remember from the past.'

Milo crouched down. 'Dom, listen to me. This is Milo. I've still got the LIZ, you know. Remember how we used to thrash up and down in her between here and Earth? Remember the time we had to race three other ships to register our strike on Lobos? You remember that race, Dom!'

The old man glanced up at him. Somehow Milo's voice seemed to calm him.

'You remember when Madeleine was born? We made record time on the return trip: I thought the old LIZ would split in two.'

Suddenly Dom Issigri spoke or rather croacked, in a voice rusty with disuse. 'Madeleine . . . little Maddy . . .'

He tugged a tattered photograph of a little girl from the pocket of his shirt.

Milo looked at it. 'There she is. About six when that was taken, wasn't she?'

'Five . . . only five . . . poor Maddy . . .' The old man sounded almost rational.

The Doctor nodded to Milo to go on.

'Do you remember that picture you had of her in a red dress. Do you still have that one, Dom. That was a good picture, that one . . .'

Confused and upset. Madeleine Issigri had come down to the tunnels to see the prisoners. She was astonished to see one of Caven's guards on duty outside the permanently locked door to her father's old study. 'Where are the prisoners?'

The guard nodded towards the door. 'All in there, safe and sound.'

'I gave orders that my father's study should be kept locked.'

The guard shrugged indifferently. 'Caven said to shove 'em in there.'

'Give me the key!'

'Chief said no one else is to go in there. Sorry miss!'

'You will be,' said Madeleine grimly.

She turned and went back the way she had come.

The guard called to his colleague who was patrolling the junction. 'Go and tell the chief that Miss Issigri's been down here trying to get in to see the prisoners. Tell him she knows where he's put them and she's in a flaming temper about it!

'Milo Clancey!' said the old man. 'It really is you, isn't it, Milo?'

'Of course it is, Dom! Come and sit down now and meet my friends.'

The old man let Milo settle him in a chair. 'Friends?' he said vaguely. 'We were friends, weren't we?'

'Of course we were, Dom – and we still are!'

The old man clutched Milo's sleeve, staring up into his face. 'He's caught you too, has he Milo? He's caught us all . . .' He looked round the little group. 'You're all going to die down here – all of you!'

12

Rocket Blast

This time it was the Doctor who managed to reassure the old man. 'We're not going to die here, Mr Issigri, and neither are you,' he said firmly. 'Now, how long have you been down here?'

The old man stared wildly at him. 'How long? I don't know – years! They came one night with guns . . . Caven and his men. They brought me down here, kept me underground like a rat.'

'That explains why he disappeared,' said Milo. 'Caven kidnapped him!'

'Why would he do that?' asked Jamie.

Milo shrugged. 'Maybe to drive a wedge between me and Madeleine – which it did, remember. If Caven wanted to get control of the company, he'd need Dom out of the way.'

'Aye, but why keep him a prisoner all this time.' Jamie lowered his voice. 'Why not just kill him?'

'He probably had his reasons,' said the Doctor

cryptically. He turned back to Dom. 'Well, Mr Issigri, we'll all just have to escape, won't we?'

'Escape? Are you mad? That door's guarded at all times, and it's the only way out of here.'

'Are you sure of that?'

'He ought to be,' said Milo glumly. 'He designed and built this room himself – cut it out of solid rock. Believe me, that door is the only way out.'

The Doctor didn't seem in the least discouraged. 'Then in that case, Mr Clancey, it's also the only way in!'

Madeleine Issigri had returned fuming to her office, and sent out a summons for Caven.

To her irritation, his assistant Dervish arrived instead, saying apologetically that Caven was temporarily unavailable.

Madeleine Issigri looked thoughtfully at him, and decided to seize her opportunity. 'You seem to be an intelligent man, Dervish, a qualified astro-engineer. How did you get mixed up with a man like Caven?'

'I was working on the space-beacon project. The budget ran into billions, and I'd got myself into debt. I . . . diverted some of the money, and Caven found out. Just one mistake, but that was enough.'

'It started as a salvage operation with me,' said Madeleine. 'After my father disappeared and I split with Milo, things were shaky for a while. Caven turned up with this salvage deal. I knew it was a bit shady, but the firm needed money. Suddenly it turned into space piracy. I didn't know what I'd got involved with – then I saw him shoot that Space

Corps man here, in my office. I've got to find a way of fighting him.'

'You can't fight Caven.'

'Not alone, perhaps, but with you to help me . . .'

'Don't even think about it,' pleaded Dervish. He saw the scornful look on her face and said angrily: 'All right, I'm scared. I know what Caven is capable of doing to us. Believe me, he'd kill us both without hesitation if he even suspected we'd been talking like this.'

'He's planning to kill the prisoners, Dervish – all of them! Are we going to let him murder four innocent people?'

'I've got to get back,' babbled Dervish. 'Lots of work to do. Just let me go, please!'

He dodged past her and headed for the door.

'You're as guilty as he is!' shouted Madeleine, but Dervish was gone.

Madeleine looked after him for a moment and came to a sudden decision.

She whirled round and headed for her vid-com console. 'Issigri Control to V-ship. Issigri Control to V-ship. Do you read me? Come in please.'

Her voice crackled faintly through the speaker on the V-ship's flight deck.

'Message from Issigri Control,' reported Penn. 'I'll put it through the amplifier.'

The voice became louder and clearer. 'Issigri Control to General Hermack. Please come in!'

Even over the airwaves Hermack could hear the edge of desperation in her voice.

'Coming up on video now, sir.'

Madeleine's anguished face appeared on the vid-com screen.

'Issigri Control to Space Corps.'

'V-Master to Issigri Control,' said Hermack. 'Receiving you now.'

'General Hermack, please listen carefully. You must come . . .'

Madeleine's voice cut off and the screen went blank.

'What the blue blazes!' growled Hermack. 'Penn, get that connection reopened!'

'It is open, sir,' reported Penn. 'Someone's pulled the plug at the other end!'

'I seem to have got back here just in time!'

One of Caven's hands was still on the cut-out switch. The other held Madeleine Issigri's wrist in a painful grip. He moved her away from the vid-com console and released her. 'Why were you trying to see the prisoners.'

'Why do you think?' Madeleine angrily rubbed her wrist. 'I was going to tell them what you were planning.'

'It seems I can't rely on you any more.' said Caven sadly.

'Maybe you'd better lock me up with the others.'

'Not yet, my dear. You've not outlived your usefulness!'

'If you think I'm going to help you now . . .'

'I think you're going to do exactly what I tell you, Madeleine. Otherwise I'll have your father flogged. I ought to tell you he's not in the best of health.'

'My father's dead!'

Caven took a photograph from his pocket. 'I assure you he's still alive. I had this taken a few days ago.'

Madeleine stared unbelievingly at the unkempt figure cringing away from the camera. 'Where is he?'

'In his study. When you ordered the place locked up it seemed the ideal place to keep him.'

'I want to see him.'

'Not yet. First, let's talk about how you're going to go on helping me. That's much more important.'

The Doctor was staring broodingly at the heavy metal door. 'That grille over the door, where does it lead to?'

'To the passage outside,' said Dom Issigri wearily. 'The steel's three inches thick. I tell you it's hopeless: I spent my first year down here working on that grille; it's hardly marked.'

'It's not another sonic lock is it, Doctor?' asked Jamie apprehensively. He could still clearly remember the Doctor's endless twanging on the tuning fork.

The Doctor looked hurt. 'Sometimes, Jamie, I think you don't really appreciate all I do for you! Mr Clancey, if we get out of this room, can you find the way back to your spaceship?'

'Once we get past the guards we'd get back easy enough. I know those tunnels like the back of me hand.'

'Excellent!' The Doctor rubbed his hands. 'Now Zoe, I want you to pass round this box of candles. Everyone take two each.'

'I'm sorry, General Hermack,' said Madeleine. 'There was a technical failure at this end.'

Hermack's face was frowning at her from the vidcom screen. 'You cut off in the middle of some urgent message.'

Madeleine was very conscious of Caven standing to one side, just out of Hermack's sight. Her objective had changed now. Instead of getting Hermack to come to Ta she wanted to keep him away, to prevent Caven from carrying out his murderous scheme. 'One of my freighter captains has just reported an attempted attack.'

'Where?'

'Just at the edge of the sector. I thought that if you tried to head off the pirates . . .'

'Too late now, they'll be out of range. We're on our way back to your planet.'

Madeleine's voice was panicky. 'No need for that, General. There's nothing wrong here, nothing at all.'

'I'm glad to hear it,' said General Hermack drily, 'however, we still have some checking up to do.'

'Very well, General. I'll have a landing pad cleared for you.'

'Thank you – and thank you for contacting us.'

As the screen went blank, Madeleine turned to Caven. 'Satisfied?'

'Yes, as it turned out. You shouldn't have tried to divert them, Madeleine. I'm counting on the return of that V-ship.' He flicked a switch on the intercome. 'Dervish, how are you getting on with that remote-control unit on Clancey's ship?'

Dervish's voice crackled back. 'I've completed the installation. I'm just running a test.'

'Good. Report back as soon as it's ready.'

Under the Doctor's direction, he and his fellow prisoners were rubbing candle-wax into the floor. They'd worn down several candles between them, and by now the whole area around the door was covered with a thin layer of wax.

The Doctor stood up. 'There, that should do it!'

He fished a cloth bag of marbles from his pocket and tipped it out over the waxed area. 'Do you think it's going to work?' asked Zoe.

'Oh, it usually does,' said the Doctor cheerfully. 'Hand me that green marble would you, Jamie?'

Jamie obeyed. 'Why this one, Doctor?'

'It's a particular favourite!' The Doctor tucked the marble into his pocket. 'Mr Clancey, are you ready?'

Milo Clancey came forward with a metal tray on which there was a sort of rat's-nest of paper and cloth. 'We ripped up one of Dom's old shirts and some aeronautical journals.'

'Splendid! That should do very nicely. Now, is everyone ready?'

Milo had broken up an old Victorian dining-chair; Jamie, Zoe, Dom and he clutched one leg each.

Jamie brandished his chair-leg. 'Aye, ready, Doctor!'

The Doctor set light to the pile of paper and rags on the tray. 'Come along the rest of you – blow!'

They all joined in, fanning and blowing on the pile of smouldering rags until it was well alight and sending up a plume of black smoke.

105

The Doctor held the tray up towards the grille over the door.

It didn't take long before the guard outside the door started sniffing suspiciously. He looked up to see smoke streaming from the grille over the door.

Muffled shouts of 'Fire! Help! Fire!' started coming from the other side of the door.

'Fire!' yelled the guard, infected by the panic. The guard at the intersection came running. 'What's happening?'

'There's a fire in there – we'd better get them out!' He fumbled with the keys at his belt.

The Doctor and his companions waited tensely.

Suddenly the door was opened.

Two guards rushed in, hit the grease and the marbles, and went down in a flailing pile of arms and legs.

They struggled to get up, but were promptly flattened by a gang of what looked like yelling demons with clubs.

'All right, quickly now,' yelled the Doctor. 'Mind you don't fall over!'

Milo took Dom's arm. 'Come on, old partner, time to go!'

Clambering over the dazed and battered guards, the Doctor and his little party disappeared down the corridor.

A few minutes later, Caven was screaming at the unfortunate guard whose bruised and battered face filled the vid-com screen in Madeleine's office.

'Useless fool – you'll be punished for this! Get

Müller and the others and get after them. You'll be lucky if you get off with being shot, you incompetent idiot!'

As the screen went blank, Caven turned to Madeleine and snarled. 'Don't imagine they can escape. There's nowhere for them to go!'

'You'll be in trouble if you haven't caught them before the Space Corps arrives, won't you?' said Madeleine fiercely.

A voice came from the intercome. 'Müller here, chief. The prisoners have been spotted heading for the old freighter dock.'

Caven thought for a moment. 'Of course . . . Listen, Müller, don't stop them, you understand? They're trying to reach Clancey's ship – so let them!'

'Understood, chief.'

Caven smiled coldly at Madeleine. 'Your friends are saving me a lot of trouble. I'll just let them blast off, then cut off the oxygen and deliver a cargo of dead space pirates to General Hermack.'

Madeleine looked at him in anguish. 'You can't do that, Caven. My father's with them!'

'Yes, I know. He'd have done better to stay where he was, wouldn't he?'

Milo dashed into LIZ 79's cabin, dragging Dom Issigri behind him. Letting the old man go, he threw himself into the pilot's seat and began a frantic instrument-check.

Seconds later the Doctor appeared, looking worriedly behind him. 'What's happened to Jamie and Zoe?'

'They waited to see if anyone was after us. Don't worry, I won't leave without them.'

Dervish's face appeared on Madeleine's vid-com screen. 'Navigation control has just picked up the V-ship on an approach path.'

'Already? Then we can't wait for Clancey to take off. Activate the override unit now, Dervish!'

'No!' screamed Madeleine. She ran at Caven, but he threw her brutally aside.

'All right, Dervish, just do as you're told!'

'I don't understand what's keeping Jamie and Zoe,' said the Doctor worriedly. 'I'd better go and hurry them up.'

'Don't be too long!' yelled Milo. 'I'm almost ready for blast-off.'

As soon as the door closed behind the Doctor, the cabin began vibrating with a low rumble of power.

'What's going on?' yelled Milo. He wrestled with the controls, but they were locked and refused to respond.

Dom Issigri looked at him in terror. 'Milo? What's happening?'

'That's the rocket drive – she's taking off by herself. The Doctor will be burned to a frazzle by the blast!'

The Doctor was tearing down the access tunnel from the launch pad. He'd started running the moment the ship started to vibrate. He didn't know what was happening – but he knew that underneath a rocket at blast-off was no place to linger. If he could only run far enough, quickly enough . . .

A shattering roar came from the launch-pad just behind him, and a blast of smoke, flames and chemical fumes ripped through the tunnel. The Doctor was picked up and hurled to the ground.

He lay motionless amid the drifting, poisonous smoke.

13

A Coffin in Space

Jamie and Zoe had been trapped at an intersection by two guards. The patrol had suddenly appeared in front of them, cutting them off from the others.

They had reached cover unseen, and there they had been forced to wait. Fortunately for Jamie and Zoe the guards got new orders over their intercoms and hurried away.

Scarcely had Jamie and Zoe resumed their journey when they felt the ground shake and heard a distant roar.

Jamie paused. 'What's that, Zoe?'

'It's the rocket motors. The Doctor's blasting off without us!'

'He wouldna do that,' said Jamie horrified. 'Come on!'

They started running in the direction of the sound.

In LIZ 79's cabin Milo wrestled with the controls.

Dom Issigri looked bewilderedly at him. 'What's happening, Milo?'

'We've walked right into Caven's trap. The ship's being operated by remote control. Caven must have installed an override unit somewhere. Now, if I could only find it . . .'

Milo reached for his tool-bag.

Gasping in the still-drifting smoke, Jamie and Zoe ran down the tunnel. They literally stumbled over the Doctor's unconscious body.

They crouched down beside him.

'Is he all right?' asked Jamie anxiously.

Zoe was feeling the Doctor's wrist. 'His pulse is pretty weak . . .'

She coughed. 'We've got to get him out of these fumes.'

Jamie heaved the Doctor over his shoulder and carried him back down the tunnels.

Madeleine watched numbly as Dervish finished linking the master control box of his remote control unit to her communications unit.

'There you are. You control the ship, the oxygen supply and the vid-com link from here.'

'Well done, Dervish,' said Caven. 'Let's take a look at them.'

Dervish adjusted the controls and a view of LIZ 79's flight cabin came up on the monitor.

Dom Issigri was slumped in a chair; Milo was busy removing a panel from the computer console.

Madeleine stared at the exhausted figure of her father scarcely able to believe he was still alive.

'All right,' said Caven gloatingly. 'Cut off their oxygen supply.'

'Please, no,' begged Madeleine. 'I'll help you, I'll give you the company – I'll do anything.' She tried to pull Dervish from the controls.

Caven brutally shoved her away. 'You heard me, Dervish. Cut the oxygen. Kill them.'

Milo was working at the computer console with frantic speed. 'It must be here somewhere. These screws have been undone and refastened recently. Hold on there, Dom!'

'It's getting very hot,' gasped the old man. 'I can hardly . . .'

Milo looked hard at the old man, then got up and went over to the air-conditioning grille. Faded ribbons were tied to it – ribbons that should have been fluttering feebly in the breeze of the air-conditioning.

They were limp and motionless.

'They're still breathing,' said Caven, sounding almost disappointed.

'There'll be oxygen in the ship for another ten minutes or so,' said Dervish.

Caven looked at Milo, who had gone back to his labours.

'Milo doesn't give up easily. He's still looking for the remote control override.'

'He won't find it,' said Dervish. 'It's all in a square inch of micro-circuits, and it's well hidden.'

They saw old Dom Issigri suddenly slip from his chair.

'Father!' gasped Madeleine.

113

'One down, one to go,' said Caven. 'Hang on a minute! What about the Doctor and his two friends? Where are they?'

Jamie had carried the Doctor to one of the bigger tunnels, where the air seemed to be flowing more freely. He gently laid the Doctor on to the rock floor. 'Come on, Doctor, wake up!'

'Take a deep breath!' urged Zoe. 'Come on, Doctor!'

The Doctor abruptly sat up – and immediately collapsed in a fit of coughing. 'Oh dear, oh dear, oh dear!' He drew a deep, gasping breath. 'That's better. Don't worry, I'm perfectly all right. I found I couldn't breath so I just stopped for a while!'

He explained how he'd come back to look for them and got caught in the rocket blast.

'But what happened?' asked Zoe. 'Why would Milo take off without us?'

'I very much doubt that he intended to, my dear.'

'Then how – oh, I see! Remote control!'

The Doctor got to his feet. 'It's the only answer. The remote control unit is probably in Issigri HQ. What we've got to do now is find it and save Milo, and Dom Issigri.'

He staggered a little and caught Jamie's arm for support.

'Steady, Doctor,' said Zoe. 'Are you sure you're all right?'

'Yes, of course I am! Don't fuss, Zoe.'

They began moving back toward Issigri HQ.

Gasping for breath, and near to collapse, Milo was still working doggedly at the console.

'He'll be unconscious in five minutes, and dead a few minutes later,' said Caven callously. 'The V-ship will arrive about seven minutes later to find a coffin in space. Nice timing, Dervish!'

Dervish looked at Madeleine Issigri's anguished face.

'Caven, do we have to go through with this? Why don't we just get away now while we've still got time?'

'General Hermack still thinks Clancey is the man he wants,' explained Caven patiently. 'So we give him Clancey – dead so he can't talk – with a load of stolen argonite in his cargo bay.'

'What about the Doctor and his friends? What if they get in touch with the Space Corps?'

Caven rose. 'They won't. I intend to find them first and take care of them. You stay here and look after our president. If she gives you any trouble – kill her!'

As soon as he was out of the room, Madeleine headed for the remote control unit.

Drawing his hand-blaster, Dervish barred her way. 'Please, I don't want to . . . but if you make me, I'll have to shoot!'

Realizing that Dervish's fear of Caven was strong enough to make him kill her, Madeleine backed away.

She looked at the screen and saw Milo slump to the floor beside her father. 'They don't stand a chance, do they? By the time the Space Corps reaches them they'll be dead.'

Dervish backed away before her reproachful eyes. 'Don't look at me like that! Don't you understand? There's nothing I can do – nothing!'

'This is your last chance to break free of Caven, Dervish. Help me! Save Milo and my father and I'll see the Space Corps goes easy on you.'

She moved towards him again and he raised the blaster. 'No, I daren't cross Caven . . . keep back!'

Madeleine saw a sudden flicker of movement at the doorway.

She circled slowly round Dervish; he moved to keep her in front of him.

'It's pointless arguing with a gutless fool like you, isn't it, Dervish. All you care about is your own skin, and you're prepared to murder helpless people to save it.'

'Shut up!' shrieked Dervish. 'Do I have to do what Caven said and kill you to shut you up?'

He raised the blaster, his face twisted with hate. For a moment Madeleine thought she had goaded him too far.

But now Dervish's back was to the door.

Jamie bounded into the room and grappled him. Dervish swung round, but Jamie knocked up his gun-hand and the energy-bolt from the blaster slammed into the remote control console. Its screen went blank. Jamie drew back a knobbly fist and knocked Dervish cold.

The Doctor and Zoe came into the room. Madeleine ran up to them. 'They've used this remote control unit to cut off the air to the LIZ. My father and Milo are dying. You've got to help them, Doctor!'

The Doctor hurried to the remote control unit, which was giving off wisps of smoke. 'I'll try, but I think the blast has fused the cables together.'

116

Producing his sonic screwdriver, the Doctor set to work . . .

No one noticed that Dervish had recovered and was crawling inch-by-inch towards the door.

Absorbed in the problem presented by the mass of charred circuits, the Doctor only gradually became aware of Jamie's voice. 'Doctor! Hey, Doctor?'

'What is it, Jamie, I'm busy.'

'That feller I clobbered – he's disappeared!'

'He's bound to warn Caven,' said Zoe.

'I'll seal the main doors, we'll be safe then,' said Madeleine. She pulled a lever on her desk and they heard the whisper of hydraulics.

To Madeleine the waiting seemed to take for ever, but it was only a minute later when the Doctor said: 'I think that's the air-supply circuit reconnected. Now, if I can just fix the radio link . . .'

A few minutes later the Doctor sat back. 'Hello, LIZ 79. Milo Clancey – Milo can you hear me?'

The ribbons tied to the air-vent in the flight cabin of LIZ 79 were fluttering feebly again.

Milo Clancey shook his head. He felt terrible – as if he had the worse hangover in the world. To make matters worse, some woman was shouting at him.

'Milo Clancey! Father! Milo! Can you hear me?'

Feebly Milo reached out and flicked a switch. 'Don't screech like that, girl, you'll ruin me speaker!'

Madeleine's joyful voice came back to him. 'Milo, is that you?'

'Give me a minute to clear the fog from me head and I'll tell you!'

'Milo, is my father all right?'

Milo rose and knelt by the body of his old friend. The scrawny chest was rising and falling, and the heartbeat was strong.

Milo went back to the controls. 'He's a tough old bird. He'll live.'

A voice boomed through the cabin. 'Milo Clancey, this is General Hermack.'

Milo clutched his temples. 'Oh, bejabers, not another one! Will you turn the volume down, general, you're blasting me eardrums!'

'Milo Clancey, we are coming alongside.'

'Will you kindly shut up for a moment, general, and let me get a word in? I've something to tell you that will curl your hair.'

Returning from his unsuccessful attempt to track down the Doctor and his friends, Caven headed towards Madeleine's office. He was just about to enter the HQ area when he ran into Dervish, who was scurrying frantically in the opposite direction.

Dervish nervously babbled his explanation. 'The Doctor and his friends attacked me. I was lucky to get away alive.'

'You're a fool, Dervish. Now they'll bring the Space Corps down on our heads. Come on!'

Dragging Dervish with him, he set off for Madeleine's office.

By now General Hermack had interrogated both Milo Clancey and Dom Issigri over the vid-com unit and, despite some initial scepticism, he was convinced that Milo's story was largely true. Now he was talking to Madeleine and the Doctor.

'Have no fear, Miss Issigri, we are coming to your assistance. We shall be making a full assault landing in exactly fifty-five minutes.'

Caven stared grimly at the heavy metal door to Issigri HQ. 'Locked. Sealed from the inside.'

He turned to the vid-com unit by the door. 'Madeleine, can you hear me? This is your old friend Caven.'

Madeleine turned from the hated features on the screen in her office. 'It's Caven, Doctor. He must be by the main door.'

She turned back to the screen. 'You can't get in, Caven. I've set the emergency locks. By the time you can cut through, the Space Corps will be here – it's preparing a landing now.'

'You're such a disappointment to me, Madeleine,' said Caven sadly. 'We were making a fortune together. Now I have to leave in an undignified hurry, and you have to stay here to die.'

'Empty threats, Caven?'

Caven dragged Dervish into the vid-com's field of view.

'Dervish here is about to visit the atomic fuel store.' He turned to the terrified figure beside him. 'You'll need about twenty charges connected up in series to do a really good job, Dervish.'

'That's madness, there isn't time. We've got to get away.'

'We shall, don't worry. Now just do as I say!'

Shoving Dervish away, Caven turned back to

119

Madeleine. 'There should be quite an explosion. I reckon it'll be equivalent to, oh, about eighty of those old-fashioned hydrogen bombs.'

'You'd never dare, Caven. You'd destroy the planet and blow yourself sky-high as well!'

'Oh, no! We're about to leave the planet by Beta Dart. I'll activate the bomb by remote control when we're a safe distance away and the V-ship is right in the flash zone.' Caven raised his hand in farewell. 'Oh, and don't try to leave, Madeleine. I've locked the doors too, from the outside. Enjoy the big bang!'

He turned away, and the screen went blank.

14

Countdown to Doom

Madeleine looked up from her control console. 'The doors are jammed all right. I don't think he was bluffing, Doctor. If he sets off an explosion in the atomic fuel store . . .'

'Then we must see that he doesn't,' said the Doctor calmly.

Like the Doctor, Jamie and Zoe had been silent while Caven made his bloodcurdling threats.

Jamie scowled ferociously. 'How do we stop him if we canna get out of here?'

'What about telling the Space Corps?' asked Zoe. 'Maybe it can get here quicker.'

The Doctor shook his head. 'V-ships are so large that they need a complicated landing procedure, and it can't be hurried. We must warn Space Corps about Caven's plan, though.'

'Aye, well who's going to get us out of here?' demanded Jamie.

'Milo Clancey,' said the Doctor simply.

Zoe frowned. 'But LIZ 79 is still stuck in orbit under remote control.'

'I know that, Zoe. But we shall free it! Madeleine, my dear, you get on to General Hermack and inform him of the situation. I'll see how Milo's getting on.'

At the core of the atomic store-room was a vast circular chamber with massive lead-shielded doors. Lining its walls in racks were the giant atomic fuel storage cylinders.

Dervish, in radiation suit, helmet and gauntlets, was clamping small atomic detonator canisters to selected cylinders. The idea was to set off a chain-reaction of atomic explosions: Caven would be satisfied with nothing less than total destruction.

He was watching Dervish now, rapping impatiently on the thick glass inspection hatch set into the door.

Dervish connected the last canister and awkwardly moved to the door.

Caven opened it to him and Dervish emerged into the stark concrete corridor outside.

When the door was closed he removed his gloves and helmet, and wiped his forehead.

'Only the detonator to connect now.' Dervish opened a metal box standing outside the door. Inside was a contraption like a complicated electronic alarm clock, which rested on a hammock of plastic webbing.

Dervish carefully lifted it out.

'You're taking your time,' snarled Caven.

'This isn't something you can hurry.'

122

'You've got to hurry! That V-ship will be dropping on us soon.' Caven looked at the clock over the door: it read 11:25. He grabbed Dervish's arm. 'We've got half an hour, Dervish!'

Dervish froze, cradling the detonator. 'If you jog my arm again, we won't have half a second. These things are ultra-sensitive. I've heard of one going up because somebody coughed!'

He carefully handed the detonator to Caven, then put on his helmet and gloves.

He took back the detonator, Caven opened the door, and Dervish went back to complete his terrifying task.

Milo Clancey, meanwhile, was trying to carry out an equally complicated task. Guided by the Doctor's voice over the space radio link, he was trying to find and disconnect the device that was controlling his ship.

The Doctor found it was rather like working by remote control. 'Now, Milo, have you found the little red wire leading into the neuristor bank?'

Milo rooted inside the computer console. 'Little red wire, he says! Haven't I found about fifty red wires? Here Dom, hold this lot out of the way, will you?'

He handed a tangle of connections to the patiently waiting Dom.

Milo peered into the interior of the console. 'Neuristor bank. Now would that be this little bunch of thingamies here . . .' He poked a finger into the console. There was a loud crackling and Milo snatched his hand away with a yell.

'It sounds as if you've found it,' said the Doctor's cheerful voice.

Milo sucked his fingers. 'Jumping galactic gobstoppers, you might have told me it was live!'

'Now then,' said the Doctor. 'Somewhere near that neuristor bank there should be the implanted override unit. It's transistorized so it'll be very small. According to Madeleine they said it was only an inch square.'

Dom Issigri peered over Milo's shoulder. The old man had been a considerable engineer in his day and the familiar surroundings of the LIZ had done much to restore him to his old self. 'I think that's it, Milo!'

'It could be,' said Milo, humouring him. 'We'll soon see!'

He grabbed the unit by its attaching wires and yanked it bodily from the console.

Immediately the LIZ gave a tremendous lurch. With a yell of mixed triumph and alarm, Milo leaped for the pilot's chair.

The Doctor's voice crackled from the speaker. 'What's happening, Milo?'

Milo was busy checking the response of the controls. 'I found it, Doctor! I found it!'

'Right,' said the Doctor, 'the next thing to do, Milo, is to dismantle it very carefully.'

Milo grinned at Dom. 'Don't worry, Doctor, I've done that as well! We're on our way back.'

Caven paced up and down the corridor. He looked up at the clock. It was 11:37.

At 11:39 the door opened and Dervish emerged, pulling off his helmet. 'All fixed.'

'Good! The ship's waiting on the launch-pad. By twelve hundred we'll be far enough away to escape the blast. Come on, let's go!'

He helped Dervish out of the radiation suit, dropping it by the door, and they hurried away. The digital display on the clock above the atomic store-room clicked from 11:39 to 11:40.

On the flight deck of the V-ship, Penn reported: 'Beta Dart on the scope, sir. Boosting off fast!'

'Caven!' said Hermack grimly. 'Get a minnow-ship, Ian, and get after him.'

'Sir!'

Warne hurried eagerly from the flight deck.

Milo beamed at Dom Issigri who lay slumped back in the co-pilot's seat. 'Just like old times, eh, Dom? You and me scuffling about in the old LIZ.'

Dom smiled feebly. 'I wish it was the old days, Milo. I was younger and stronger then.'

He shook his head, trying to clear a sudden dizziness.

Milo shot him a worried look. 'Hold on, Dom, a few minutes more and we'll be back on Ta and you'll see your Maddy again.'

'Maddy,' murmured Dom Issigri, and it was as if the name gave him strength. 'I'll be all right, Milo.'

'That's me boy! Hold tight now, I'm on the approach orbit!'

'I'm right on the Beta Dart's tail, sir,' reported Warne. 'Thirty seconds and I'll be within missile range.'

'Well done, Ian,' said Hermack exultantly. 'Stand by – don't fire until I give the word. I'm still not sure of the situation on Ta . . .'

A strange voice cut through on the communications channel. 'Beta Dart to V-ship! This is Caven. I can tell you the situation, general. I've got the Issigri atomic fuel store wired for an explosion that will destroy the planet. At this distance it will take out both our ships as well.'

'Miss Issigri told me about your murderous plan, Caven. You must be mad. You'd better surrender now . . .'

'Oh no, general. You'd better get that minnow off my tail, because if it comes any closer I'll pull the switch *now* and we'll all die together!'

There was a click as Caven broke off communication.

'Better drop back, Ian. Don't lose him, but don't get too close.'

'Understood, sir!'

Hermack looked up at the flight deck clock. It read 11:48. 'Twelve minutes,' muttered Hermack. He raised his voice. 'Penn, get me Issigri HQ.'

'LIZ 79 to Issigri HQ, can you hear me?'

Madeleine's voice came through the speaker. 'We hear you, Milo. Where are you?'

'We'll be seeing you in a few minutes. We've just landed.'

He could hear the tension in Madeleine's voice. 'Thank goodness! Please come to Issigri HQ and release us. There isn't much time, Milo!'

'On my way, Maddy!' Milo heaved himself out of the pilot's seat and looked dubiously at his old friend. 'Better stay here I think, old partner. I've got some running to do, and I don't think you're quite up to it!'

Dom nodded feebly. 'Hurry, Milo!'

Milo Clancey hurtled from the cabin. Seconds later Dom heard him clattering down the ladder.

Madeleine was talking to General Hermack on the vid-com. 'Milo's on his way to release us. As soon as he gets here, the Doctor's going to the atomic store room to try to defuse the detonator.'

Hermack's face was grave. 'I estimate that by twelve hundred hours Caven's Beta Dart will be safely out of range. He'll set off the explosion anyway then – he'll have nothing to lose. I shall order Major Warne to launch a missile attack at twelve hundred hours precisely, Miss Issigri. I'm sorry but I have no alternative.'

Milo threw open the doors to Madeleine Issigri's office and leaned panting by the door. 'I haven't run so far or so fast since . . .'

He broke off because the Doctor, Madeleine, Zoe and Jamie were all sprinting past him out of the door.

'Hey, where are you going?' he shouted.

'To turn off a bomb,' yelled Jamie over his shoulder.

'A bomb?' Milo drew a deep breath and pounded wearily after the others.

Major Warne was speaking quietly over the vid-com. 'I'm still on Caven's tail, sir. I could creep the minnow in, get off a missile salvo before they knew what hit them.'

Hermack was tempted for a moment. Then he shook his head. 'No, we'll wait, Ian. They've got . . .' He glanced at the clock. 'They've still got seven minutes.'

Milo and Madeleine were bundling the Doctor into Dervish's discarded anti-radiation suit.

Madeleine looked up at the clock. 'You've got six minutes, Doctor.'

They lowered the helmet over the Doctor's head. His muffled voice said: 'Open the door, Jamie.'

Jamie opened the door to the atomic storage area, and the Doctor went inside.

The detonator looked like a great metal spider, thought the Doctor, its metal body crouching in the centre of the room, power cables stretching out from it like long silvery legs.

The Doctor studied the problem for a moment.

The leads were firmly fastened at either end. It was impossible to cut them without power tools and there was no time for that. There was little time for anything in six – the Doctor looked at the clock above the door – no, five minutes.

Producing his sonic screwdriver, the Doctor began unscrewing the top of the detonator unit.

Jamie, Zoe, Madeleine and Milo jostled round the inspection window to see what the Doctor was doing.

He had got the lid off the detonator and was staring inside.

128

'He's no doing anything at all,' reported Jamie.

'Come on, Doctor, hurry!' whispered Zoe.

'He has to find the right wire,' explained Milo. 'If he cuts the wrong one, he could set the thing off!'

They saw the Doctor reach inside the detonator unit . . .

Hermack looked at the clock.

11:57.

The seconds ticked by.

'One hundred and fifty seconds to zero, sir,' reported Penn.

Hermack was in an impossible situation. If he left it too late, Caven would set off the bombs as soon as he felt safe, destroying most of the planet Ta, and the V-ship with it. But if Hermack fired too early and Caven spotted the missiles . . .

'We'll have to risk it,' said Hermack softly. Raising his voice he shouted: 'Attack, Ian, attack!'

The minnow-ship sped forwards on a converging course with the sleek black Beta Dart . . .

The Doctor was gingerly lifting a thin metal cylinder from the middle of a nest of circuits inside the detonator. The cylinder was connected by two thin wires: one green, one red.

They would have to be severed – in the right order.

11:59. 'Fire!' shouted General Hermack.

Twin torpedos streaked from the nose cone of the minnow-ship, converging upon the Beta Dart.

Caven saw the missile tracks on the radar screen in the cockpit of the Beta Dart. 'I warned you, Hermack,' he shouted, and reached for the detonator switch.

'No,' screamed Dervish. 'We're still in the blast area! We'll be killed!'

He tried to drag Caven away from the switch.

The Doctor came to a decision and snapped first the green wire, then the red.

Caven hurled Dervish aside. 'We'll all die together, Hermack – now! He threw the detonator switch.

Nothing happened . . .

Not until Warne's Martian missiles struck, blowing the Beta Dart into flaming fragments.

The Doctor sighed deeply, tossed the detonator core aside and walked slowly out of the atomic storage room to where a jubilant Jamie and Zoe were waiting.

'Apparently the Space Corps destroyed the Beta Dart seconds after the Doctor defused the detonator,' said Madeleine.

They were all back in her luxurious office celebrating their victory in the finest Venusian champagne.

'Well, at least those Space Corps boys did something right for once,' rumbled Milo. 'Where is Hermack anyway?'

'He'll be landing any minute,' said Madeleine. 'Apart from anything else, he's got to arrest me and take me back to Earth for trial. I'm a space pirate, remember.'

'An ex-space pirate,' said Milo firmly. 'Me and Dom will have something to say about that.'

Madeleine smiled at him. 'Don't worry. General Hermack says they won't be too hard on me. My father's evidence will help.' She stood up. 'He's still on the LIZ, so I think I must go and see him.'

She came over to the Doctor and kissed him on the cheek. 'Thank you for all your help, Doctor. You've been wonderful, all of you.' She hurried out.

'Doctor, what about the TARDIS?' asked Zoe.

'Aye, where is it?' said Jamie. 'I've fair lost track of it!'

'The TARDIS is currently orbiting Lobos, Mr Clancey's home planet, inside one of the other beacon fragments!'

Madeleine Issigri suddenly reappeared in the doorway. 'I forgot to tell you, Milo . . . General Hermack's orders are that you and the Doctor are to stay here until he arrives on Ta. He wants a long full statement from you both.'

She went out; the Doctor and Milo looked at each other.

Then Milo rose. 'No doubt you're keen to be getting back to this TARDIS of yours, Doctor?'

The Doctor got up too. 'I most certainly am, Mr Clancey.'

'Well, I have to be getting back to Lobos myself. Could I offer you a lift in the LIZ?'

'That's very kind of you, Mr Clancey.'

'Would right now be a convenient time at all?'

'Right now would be perfect,' said the Doctor. 'Jamie, Zoe, come along now!'

'What about General Hermack?' protested Zoe.

'Aye, he'll be furious,' said Jamie.

'Exactly!' said the Doctor and Milo together, and hurried out.

Zoe shook her head. 'Like a couple of naughty children!'

'A lift in the LIZ, eh?' said Jamie gloomily. 'I'm not sure I wouldn't rather walk.'

Zoe grinned. 'It may come to that yet. Come on Jamie!'

They hurried after the Doctor and Milo.

Just as the V-ship completed its cumbersome landing procedure, Penn reported: 'Ship taking off from Ta!'

Major Warne looked at the radar screen.

'Surely that's Milo Clancey's LIZ, sir?'

General Hermack turned to the communicator. 'Clancey? Milo Clancey? You are to return to Ta immediately! That is an order!'

Only a crackling of static came back over the speaker. That and a strange sound no one could quite identify.

As Major Warne said later, it sounded very like an old-fashioned raspberry . . .

THE COMPLETE ADVENTURES
– IN PRINT!

**Target Books have published novels
based on just about all the Doctor Who
stories ever shown on television – plus a
few that never quite made it to the
screen. Almost 150 books in all – and
most of them are still available.**

**Ask for Target Books at your bookshop
– and if you would like an up-to-date
list of Doctor Who novels, please send a
large stamped addressed envelope to:**

**The Doctor Who Editor
WH Allen & Co. Plc
175-179 St John Street
London EC1V 4LL**